RIP CURRENT

THE GRAYTON SERIES

JILL SANDERS

GRAYTON

For Beautiful Hawaii
Mahalo

SUMMARY

Cole is used to fame and has had his fill of women who fall at his feet, but the one woman he desires the most shows nothing but disdain for him and his reckless ways.

Wendy can't stand Cole, at least in her head. Her body and heart, on the other hand, desire him beyond anything else.

Wendy leaned against the bar and sighed. She tried not to let her eyes wander to where her new boss's three brothers stood watching people walk in the front door. It was grand opening day of the Boardwalk Bar and Grill, and she felt a shiver of nerves run up her spine. But it had nothing to do with the crowd of people she heard waiting outside. No, the cause of all of her anxiety stood just a few feet away in cut-off jean shorts, a teal green tank top, and the most worn-out pair of flip-flops she'd ever seen.

His hair was blond, and, unlike his brothers' darker locks, he kept his long and unkempt. In fact, he didn't look anything like the other two men crowded around him.

The doors opened, and the trio stood watching women in small bikinis walk into the restaurant. All three of them had grins on their faces as they slowly sipped on drinks.

If there's one thing she'd learned bartending the last few years, it's that what a person drank said a lot about them. For example, Marcus, the oldest of the three boys, leaned against the wall sucking down a Bud Light. The beer meant he was a hard worker and appreciated just having a cold, cheap beer slide down his throat. His dark hair was messy, and his clothes looked like he had worn them while he'd been sawing and painting.

Roman, the middle of the three, stood with his back straight and his eyes taking in everything. He was wearing a suit and tie, but he still stared at every blonde woman who walked in the door. For him, it was a tall Guinness. He was used to nice things and didn't mind working hard to get them.

Cole. She sighed when her eyes roamed over the blond god of her dreams, who was leaning lazily against a chair as he joked with his brothers. Most men would be self-conscious to be holding a fruity drink with an umbrella in it. Not Cole. Piña coladas were all he'd ordered since she'd first met him days before the opening. Which meant he was comfortable with who he was.

It was no wonder that every woman who walked in the door zeroed in on him. After all, the man was plastered on billboards all over the world. Half-naked, no less. And not only was Cole Grayton a famous surfer-slash-model, he was sexy as hell.

It annoyed Wendy that Cole got all the attention from the ladies without even trying.

Over the next few hours, she was the busiest she'd ever been. When Alan whizzed by her and flipped a bottle in two quick turns, cheers erupted from a small group of women sitting at the bar. She smiled over at him and shook her head. He smiled back at her and winked as he tossed a bottle behind his back and caught it in front of him to even more cheers.

"Show off," she murmured as she finished building a Guinness.

When Cassey had made her bar manager, the first thing she'd done was hire on her best friend from the last two years. Alan was the best bartender she'd worked with and a good friend from her last job just down the coast. Together, they were the best bartending team along the Emerald Coast.

"You going to watch him all night or get me another drink, sweetheart?"

She turned, and her entire body stiffened. Cole leaned against the bar, smiling at her with his perfect teeth. She felt as if her feet were suddenly glued to the floor.

She couldn't stop the frown from growing on her lips as she looked at him. He was too perfect. No man should ever be given this much power over women. Ever.

"I would have thought that you'd have a row of women offering to buy you your girlie drinks." She turned and pushed the Guinness towards the owner. The glass slid down the bar and landed perfectly in the hands of Cole's brother, who smiled and winked back at her. She liked Roman and Marcus. It was hard not to. But Cole…she felt that familiar flutter rush down her legs just thinking his name. Cole did something to her that she wasn't ready to own up to just yet.

He chuckled and leaned a little closer. "Are you offering?"

She closed her eyes and sighed. "Buddy, wrong tree." She turned and started building his frou-frou drink. Not that she had anything against piña coladas; hell, she would suck a few down tonight if she wasn't working.

When she turned to hand him his drink, she stopped.

He'd been staring at her. Not just looking but staring. Hard. Instantly, her legs felt weak and her heart did a quick somersault in her chest. Damn, she was going to have to watch herself around this guy.

Setting his drink down, he tried to toss a bill on the bar. She shoved it back in his hand. "You're the boss's brother." She nodded to where Cassey stood on a small landing, overlooking everything. "She'll have my head if you pay me."

Cole smiled. "I don't take you for the kind of person who is afraid of anything."

She pasted on her best smile and leaned closer to him. She watched his eyes zero in on her ample chest and felt a little self-reward. "Big boy, I'm not afraid of men who drink piña coladas." She leaned back and watched his smile grow.

"That's because you've never been with a man who knows what he likes and isn't afraid to take it." He winked and then slowly made his way back to his brothers, who had taken over the largest booth near the back. She frowned as she noticed that it was now filled with single women who, no doubt, were all fighting to see who would get to go home with the famous Cole Grayton.

She couldn't stop herself from watching him go or from dreaming, for just a moment, about what it would be like.

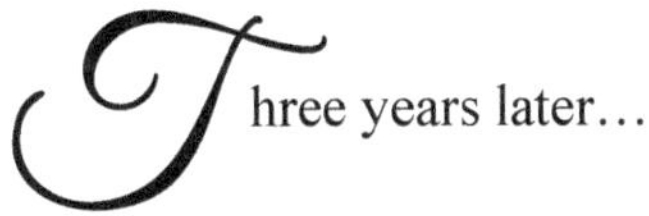hree years later…

Cole walked into his sister's bar and winced. Even though it had been almost a year since his motorcycle accident, he still felt pain shooting up his hip when he stood for too long. Not even his family knew about this new predicament. They'd been told about the broken collarbone and arm at the hospital. His hip hadn't started hurting until weeks after he'd laid his bike down thanks to the cab driver who'd flipped a U-turn right in front of him.

He winced again at the pain and decided he couldn't get off his feet fast enough. Making a beeline towards the bar, he frowned when he noticed Wendy wasn't behind it. Instead, busy as always, was the man he was the most jealous of in life.

Walking over, he propped his bad hip up on the stool and waited until Alan walked over to him.

"Your usual?"

He shook his head. "No, give me a shot of Jameson."

"Bad day?" Alan leaned against the bar and looked at him.

He nodded. "You could say that."

What did Wendy see in the guy? Sure, most people would probably think he was good-looking; he'd heard a lot of women say how much the guy looked like Vin Diesel. Alan certainly had more muscles than Cole did, at least at the moment. He frowned a little and thought about using some of his brother's weights when he got back home.

Alan was an ex-marine, which gave the guy an extra boost around the women. He was always entertaining them with stories of his time in the service. Is that what Wendy liked about the guy? They were always laughing and flirting with each other.

"Want a chaser with that?" Alan turned to grab a glass and looked over his shoulder at Cole. "I just made a new batch of Bushwacker."

Cole sighed. He couldn't turn down his favorite chocolaty drink. "Sure." He scooted up onto the stool and almost moaned when the weight was lifted from his hip. His arm and collarbone had healed quickly with no side effects, but he wondered if he'd damaged his hip beyond repair. "Wendy working tonight?" He tried not to glance around the room.

"Naw, she's got the weekend off." Alan glanced at him. "Your sister is upstairs though." He nodded to the stairs that led up to Cassey's office.

His sister had taken last month off after marrying Luke Callaway. The two of them had hightailed it to Hawaii for their honeymoon. He'd been a little jealous of them enjoying the waves in the photos they'd sent everyone, so he'd set up a photo shoot for himself off the North Shore.

It had been wonderful—peace and quiet and big waves. But two days into his trip, word had gotten out to the tourists that he was in town. All of a sudden, the beaches were flooded with competitive surfers who wanted to show him up and half-naked girls trying to get his attention, and his quiet time had turned into a circus. He was so bored of it all that he'd packed up and headed home early.

"Thanks. I'll wait until she comes down to make her rounds."

Alan smiled. "Might be a while. Luke showed up just before you did."

Cole chuckled. "Then I guess it's a good thing I'm not heading up there."

Alan laughed and set his drinks in front of him.

"Where'd she go?" he asked before the man could tend to someone else.

Alan tilted his head in question.

"Wendy?" he mumbled.

"Oh, um, she said something about needing a break and heading to her sister's place close to the Florida-Alabama border."

Cole nodded and swallowed the Jameson quickly. He was grateful for the chocolate chaser that cleared the sting a little. He swiveled on the stool and glanced around the bar, thinking about Wendy. He hadn't known she had a sister. He'd known her for over three years now, and he couldn't list five things about her other than the fact that she caused his heart to race and his libido to skyrocket.

She was the only woman, other than his sister, who hadn't fallen for his shit. Most women swooned at his feet when they realized who he was. Not Wendy. She'd always been cool and calm, with enough flirt in her to leave him full of desire.

He glanced over at Alan and wondered if the rumors were true about the pair. All his sister ever said about her bar manager was that Cole should stay away from her.

Cassey was too loyal. A few minutes later, he chuckled as he watched his sister walk down the stairs, hand in hand with her new husband. Good thing he hadn't surprised them upstairs. His sister's hair was loose from its long braid, and Luke had the look of a man who had just gotten everything he'd ever wanted.

Cole sighed and dreamed of the day he would feel something close to that. He'd had plenty of women in the past, but he'd been on a hiatus ever since his motorcycle accident. Something about that day had caused him to pause and look at his life. He'd had plenty of scares in the past, but nothing that had caused his life to flash before his eyes. Even when he'd almost drowned off the southern coast of Africa, he'd never experienced anything like it before.

"Hey." Cassey walked up and took the Coke Alan had set down for her.

"Hey." He smiled and pulled his sister close and hugged her next to him. "Your shirt's on inside out."

He chuckled when she gasped and looked down quickly.

"You're terrible." She swatted his shoulder.

"Just the fact that you looked tells me what you two were up to." Luke shook his hand, still smiling ear to ear.

"You're just jealous," Cassey said, sitting on the stool next to him and sighing.

He nodded. "Yeah, who wouldn't want to get their hands on this big guy." He slapped Luke on the back and laughed.

Cassey just shook her head and smiled. "He's all mine. Besides, what happened to…" Her eyebrows lifted as she thought about his last girl's name. Hell, even he couldn't remember the sultry brunette's name.

"We broke it off." He shrugged his shoulders and motioned for Alan to give him another shot and chaser.

"What are you drinking?" Cassey grabbed his glass and sniffed. "Whiskey?" She frowned at him. "Why are you drinking whiskey?" She held the glass away from Alan before he could pour another.

"Because it goes so well with Bushwackers." He held up his other glass and sipped the last of the frozen drink down.

"Whiskey and Bushwackers?" Cassey made a face, causing him to laugh.

"Stick to your Cokes." He tapped the can of soda she'd set down at the bar. "Leave the heavy stuff to us men."

She shook her head. "Why are you drinking the heavy stuff?" She set the glass down and crossed her arms over her chest.

"Maybe I needed it." He took the glass and swallowed the whiskey down quickly, trying not to cringe in front of his sister. He really did hate liquor. That's why he usually stuck to the fruity drinks. When he took a large swallow of the chocolate drink, he felt a little better.

"What's going on?" She frowned up at him.

"Maybe he doesn't want to talk about it," Luke chimed

in before taking a swig of his beer and running a hand up Cassey's arm.

Cassey frowned even more and shook her head. "No, I can see it now. Your eyes are dull."

He chuckled. "Thanks."

She shook her head again. "You're in pain." She gasped. "Where?" She set her drink down and started running her hands over his chest and arms.

He started to laugh and grabbed her hands. "Damn it, Cass, you know I'm ticklish." Then his eyes moved to the doorway and his smile increased.

"Are you?" Cassey chuckled, but he couldn't take his eyes off the doorway. "There, now you have the sparkle back in your eyes," his sister said, taking his chin in her hands and forcing his face towards hers.

Wendy was bored out of her mind. Not that her little sister wasn't fun, but she hadn't expected to be sitting in her apartment on Friday night, watching a movie while her sister made out with her current boyfriend.

They had planned a weekend full of fun and sister time, but then Willow's boyfriend Justin—or was it, Jacob? —had shown up and asked if he could crash there since he'd been kicked out of his apartment by his buddies who had girls over.

Less than five minutes into the movie, Wendy jumped off the sofa and grabbed her purse and bag.

"Where are you going?"

"Out."

"I thought you were going to stay the whole weekend."

"That was before." She looked over at Jacob or whatever his name was. "I'll catch you next week."

"Oh." Willow glanced at her boyfriend and Wendy could tell she was torn.

"It's okay, really. I had a few things to do anyway." Wendy smiled.

"Okay. I'm still planning on coming over to your place next month for the concert."

"Sure." She nodded, knowing her sister would probably flake on that too. "See you then."

The drive back to Surf Breeze was short, even with all the tourists crowding the main roads. When she stopped in front of her little condo, she sighed. It was still early enough that she was dying for entertainment. Being a bartender for almost five years had set her internal clock on permanent night mode. If she went into her condo now, she knew she'd be bored out of her mind. That, or she'd find herself cleaning. She shivered at that thought.

"Fine!" She banged her hands on the steering wheel of her Jeep. "I'll swing in to Cassey's and if no one is there, I'll take a nice long walk on the beach." She sighed and swung her legs out of the open side of the Jeep. She loved taking the doors off her Jeep during the summer months. If she could, she'd drive with them off year-round, but this last winter had gotten way too cold for it.

It was a short walk to the bar. She loved taking the boardwalk and enjoyed the hustle and bustle that marked the middle of the summer months. By the time she walked in the front doors of the bar and grill, there was a bead of sweat dripping down the middle of her back.

She had just stepped in the doorway when she heard his deep laugh and stopped dead. Her heart did the same little jump it always did when she saw him, but this time there was a quick pang near the end. She thought about turning around and walking back out, but he'd already seen her and she didn't want to be childish.

Especially since the last time she'd seen him, she'd… She closed her eyes quickly and took a deep breath. She was not going to stoop to his level. Holding her head up high, she walked towards the bar.

"Wendy?" Cassey smiled. "I thought you were spending the weekend at Willow's?"

She stopped next to her friend and boss. "I was until Justin showed up." She sighed. "Or was his name Jacob?" She tilted her head and tried to remember.

"Oh, trouble in paradise? I thought your sister was happy with this one," Cassey said, hugging her a little.

"She is. A little too happy." She leaned over the bar and grabbed a bottle of beer, not really noticing or caring what kind it was. Using the side of the bar, she flipped the top off and took a swig.

"Well, you're just in time." Cassey smiled. "We're going to have some dinner. Oh, look, here come Marcus and Shelly." She turned in time to see the couple walk in. Marcus's arm was wrapped around the blonde shop owner's shoulders. Both of them were smiling and laughing as they walked in.

Wendy really liked Shelly. Not only did the woman have style, but she was also very down to earth. It was hard to find locals Wendy could stand to be in the same room with for more than five minutes. Shelly was one of those people.

"Hey," Marcus said, stopping right in front of the

growing group. "Looks like we're just in time for the party."

"Where's Roman?" Cassey asked, looking around.

Cole jumped in. "He had some business in Atlanta. Said he'd be gone for a few weeks."

Cassey frowned. "Why didn't he tell us?"

Wendy saw Cole shrug his shoulders and walk towards her. When he flopped his arm around her shoulders, much like his brother was doing to his fiancée, she glared at him until he dropped his arm and smiled at her.

"I didn't ask. Besides, he's a big boy and now I've got the place all to myself for a while." He threw his arm over her shoulders again. She tried to control the excitement that rushed through her as he started to play with the ends of her hair.

"I should give him a call…" Cassey reached for her phone, only to have her husband tug on her arm. "He'll call if he needs us. Let's eat. I'm starved."

"Yeah, Cass, your man worked up an appetite." Cole smiled brightly and started walking her towards the back booth that they always inhabited. Cassey hit Cole's shoulder playfully as they walked towards the back.

The fact that Cole's arm was still around her shoulders made her feel a little antsy. And it only heightened her anxiety when he sat next to her, especially when his thigh rubbed up against hers.

"I'm glad you came back," he whispered next to her ear. His hand went to her thigh and she felt a shiver run straight from that point to the apex in her legs.

Damn. The man had too much power over her body.

She shifted a little, trying to slide farther away from him, but only ended up pushing herself against the wall with him next to her. He chuckled a little at her move, so she glared at him.

"You're squishing me," she said under her breath.

"Me?" He looked at her innocently. She wasn't buying it. "You're the one trying to become wallpaper." He smiled and threw his arm over her shoulders and began playing with her hair again.

"I thought you were going to visit your sister this weekend?" Shelly broke in.

"It was called off due to Willow's new beau crashing the party."

"Oh, I'm sorry. I know how much you were looking forward to the break."

She nodded, not trusting her voice since Cole's hand was still on her thigh.

"Problems at work? Or is it more on a personal level?" Cole asked, glancing towards the bar.

She glared at him and shoved her elbow into his ribs. "Neither."

He frowned and she felt him stiffen a little beside her. The conversation turned towards the house Marcus and Shelly were remodeling. Marcus knew how to make any story funny and by the time their food arrived, everyone around the table was laughing hard.

"So, that's the last night I'll believe him when he says his workers won't be there in the morning and the last time I'll sleep au naturel. At least until his buddies are done working on our place," Shelly broke in with a smile.

"What about you?" Cole whispered towards her.

"What about me?" She glanced at him, her smile faltering a little as she shoved a grilled shrimp in her mouth.

He leaned closer and his smile grew. "Have any special sleeping habits you'd like to pass on?"

She held back a chuckle. "Yeah." She leaned a little closer and whispered right next to his ear. "I snore." Then she sat up and popped another shrimp into her mouth and tried to ignore his sexy laugh.

CHAPTER 2

$\mathcal{C}$ole tried everything in his power, short of begging, to persuade Wendy to let him walk her home. The two shots of whiskey earlier had given him just enough courage to actually flirt with her, something he'd never allowed himself to do before.

Since women usually fell at his feet, most people assumed that he was a smooth talker around the opposite sex. Not true. Actually, Marcus was the smooth one. Roman had the dashing good looks. Cole was just… well, Cole. He'd always felt awkward around women. Maybe that's why he tended to date whoever showed the most interest, or whomever he picked from the line of ladies that followed him around.

He glanced over at Wendy, who was walking next to him in silence. He found it especially hard to be around her. He always felt tongue-tied. Even now, as they walked the few blocks to her condo, he couldn't think of anything to say to her.

It had been almost a week since they'd argued about

his reckless ways, and he'd been desperate to see her since then. After their fight, he'd followed her from her place at the bar to the refrigerator where she was getting a fresh supply of limes. When she'd turned back around to yell at him, he'd bumped into her and had swooped in without thinking and kissed her. Hard and fast.

He'd been so shocked by his actions that he'd made a quick retreat without saying anything more. Since then, he'd been avoiding her. Until tonight. Maybe it was the Jameson? Who was he kidding; the two shots had worn off hours ago.

Sighing, he decided to blurt out the first thing that came to mind. "I didn't know you had a sister."

She glanced at him and slowed her steps a little. "Willow is my half-sister. Almost eight years younger." She sighed and shoved her hands into her pockets. "I'd kind of hoped that this weekend would be a bonding experience." She glanced off towards the water. It was too dark to see the surf, but they could hear the low waves lapping at the sugar sand. "My father left us to fend for ourselves, even when he was around, but when he left for good…" She stopped and sighed, then walked over to the railing near the steps that led down to the beach. "Want to head down for a while?" She nodded towards the water.

He shrugged his shoulders. "You're not in a hurry to get home?"

She chuckled. "I'm used to late hours. Actually, for me, it's the middle of my work shift."

He smiled and then held out his arm for her to take. She glanced at it, then shrugged a little and wrapped her arm through his.

"This is nice," she said as they slipped off their sandals and left them by the steps.

He glanced at her in question.

"Us, not at each other's throats for a change."

He chuckled. "I could always do something stupid to piss you off."

She smiled and shook her head. "You do have a knack for being quite audacious."

"And you have a knack for always trying to set me straight." He took her hand and started walking towards the surf. "Why do you suppose that is?"

He felt her tense, but the closer they got to the water, the more she relaxed. Her hand felt good in his. So good… perfect, actually.

"I guess I can see a lot of my father in you."

"Oh? Does he surf or model men's underwear?" He smiled.

She chuckled and shook her head no. "He's a biker."

His eyebrows shot up. "Like Lance Armstrong stuff?"

She laughed and he enjoyed the sexy sound coming from her lips. "No, like in Hell's Angels."

"Oh." He smiled. "There's nothing wrong with riding a hog. I've got one…" He frowned when he remembered his bike was sitting at a wreck-yard somewhere because of his accident.

"Yeah." She frowned over at him, dropped his hand, and stepped back. "I remember."

He shook his head. "It could have been worse. Besides, it wasn't my fault." He turned towards her and took her shoulders in his hands, pulling her closer to him. Again, he felt her tense.

"So, you've said." She sighed. "I don't want to start an argument."

He smiled. "Good, then don't." He leaned a little closer to her.

"Cole." She shook her head. "I can't… I don't want…"

He didn't let her get any further. He'd been holding back his feelings for her for too long, and he didn't give a damn any longer if she had anything going with the muscle-bound bartender or not.

When their lips touched, he couldn't stop the sigh from escaping. It was nothing like their first kiss.

Last time, the kiss had been fueled by anger. Now there wasn't anything between them except the desire he felt running through his entire body.

He pulled her closer and felt her shiver next to him. Her hands went up to his shoulders, and he felt a quick tug of exhilaration rush through him. His hands traveled over her body, enjoying her soft hips as he settled on the place that had driven him nuts for years—her sweet little arse.

"You feel so good," he moaned next to her heated skin.

She sighed as he ran his mouth down her neck and reached the top of her silk shirt. He wanted to tug the soft material off her in one quick motion but knew this wasn't the time or place for it.

Instead, he pulled her down to the soft sand and lay beside her. He ran his hands over her body slowly as he kissed her until he felt her breath hitch.

"Cole?" She sighed. "This really isn't a good idea."

"Sure, it is." He smiled as he reached up to brush a strand of her long blonde hair away from her face. "Every now and then it's okay to do something reckless."

She shook her head and sighed, then pushed on his

shoulders until he leaned back. She sat up a little. "I can't afford to be reckless."

He leaned back on his elbows in the warm sand and looked at her. The light from the boardwalk was shining behind her head, making her blonde hair look illuminated.

She tucked her legs up to her chest and wrapped her arms around them tightly.

"Why not?"

She closed her eyes. "I promised myself I wouldn't turn out like my dad. I need stability. I need to know what tomorrow is going to hold."

He chuckled. "Pretty boring if you ask me."

Her eyes flew open and she looked down at him. "And that's why this isn't a good idea."

She rested her chin on her knees and looked off to where the moon was resting over the water.

"I'm a pretty stable guy—" he started to say, but her burst of laughter stopped him.

Wendy glanced over at Cole and stopped laughing when she saw the face he was making. "Really?" She dropped her arms from her knees and looked at him more closely. "You're the most unstable person I know."

He was silent for a while and she wondered if she'd crossed the line.

"Your dad must have hurt you really bad." He reached over and ran a finger up her thigh. She felt the heat from him zip up her leg.

She tried to act casual about it and shrugged. "He

wasn't really around a lot. Actually, no one was around a lot when I was younger."

"What about your sister?"

She looked at him, then down at his hand as it played over her knee. The fact that she was wearing shorts, giving him access to her skin, didn't go unnoticed by either of them. She'd lost track of what he'd asked her. Her mind refused to think about anything other than the feeling of his hand on her leg.

"What about her?" Her voice sounded strained a little.

"Someone must have been around with the kid. What about your stepmom?"

She sighed. "Carrie wasn't the mother type. When Willow was seven, she was picked up for shoplifting. It was the last offense in a very long line that sent her away for a few years. When she got out…" She shrugged. "We never heard from her."

"Where was your dad?"

"Riding with his gang. He'd send a postcard or an envelope of money to help pay the rent, but for the most part, he was on the road."

"How old were you?" he asked, frowning.

"Fifteen when he left. Seventeen when he returned."

"Returned?"

"After he… found out about the cancer." She looked at him. She wished she could deny that it still stung. "Less than six months later, we spread his ashes in the ocean."

"I'm sorry." He tugged on her until she lay back down next to him. His hand went into her hair. "I'm not like him, you know."

"From where I'm standing, you're from the same mold," she said under her breath.

"I've got one of the best families in the world. They see me often and I'm always around." He smiled. "Besides, if I was gone too long, who would you have to fight with?"

She smiled and wrapped her arms around him. "There are lots of people that come in. I can choose whomever I want to argue with."

Cole frowned. "Are you trying to start a fight now?"

She giggled and shook her head. "Why would you care?"

She hadn't even gotten out the last words before his mouth was covering hers again. This time, there was more heat behind his lips as they moved slowly over hers.

She'd dreamed about him, just like this. His first kiss, in the freezer, had left her branded and desperate for more. Now, as his hands rushed over her, she desperately wished that she could forget who he was and what he stood for. But even when he pulled back and looked down at her with those incredible blue eyes, she couldn't forget.

"Cole, I…"

He sighed and closed his eyes, then rested his forehead on hers. "I know…" He sighed. "Come on." He stood up quickly and held out his hand for her. "I'll walk you home like I promised my sister I would."

She took his hand and allowed him to pull her up, then busied herself by dusting the soft sand from her shorts and legs as he watched. They walked in silence for a while as she replayed their conversation in her head.

"You know; I didn't mean to make you sound bad." She glanced at him as they turned down her street.

"I know."

"It's just that I really want stability in my life."

"I know," he said again and took her hand in his. "But sometimes what you want and what you need are two different things."

She couldn't stop the burst of laughter from slipping out of her lips. "What makes you believe that?" She stopped in front of her door, her keys in her hands.

He smiled and leaned against her front railing. "Invite me in and I'll tell you."

She chuckled. "That's probably the worst idea I've heard yet."

His smile grew. "Won't know until you give it a try."

She shook her head, but she couldn't stop herself from smiling. "You're different tonight."

She watched his smile falter as he leaned his hip against her railing. "Maybe I'm trying to turn over a new leaf."

She leaned against the door frame and sighed. "It's about time."

He chuckled. "Didn't like the old Cole?"

She sighed again. "It isn't that I didn't like him, just that I couldn't stand to be in the same room with him." She smiled.

"Ouch." He put his fist up to his chest and beat it a few times. "Hurts right here."

"Thanks for walking me home." She started to open her door. He took two steps and was beside her. His hands went to her arms as he turned her towards him.

"How about going sailing with me tomorrow?"

She blinked a few times. "You don't have a boat." She frowned.

"My family does. Up on the bay. I was going to go fishing all by myself, but since you have the weekend off, I thought we could make a day of it. Then we can cook up what we catch for dinner."

"I…" She shook her head and started to make some excuse, but he broke in.

"Before you say no"—his fingers flexed gently on her arms— "what if I promise to be the new Cole. No sign of the old one all day." The porch light caused his eyes to gleam. His face was really something to look at, especially in the soft light.

She thought about what she was going to do for the rest of the weekend, now that her sister had chosen her boyfriend over her. The only thing that came to mind, besides thoroughly cleaning her condo, was watching every episode of Breaking Bad on Netflix. Did she really want to spend an entire weekend moping around feeling lonely and sorry for herself?

"Okay, why not. I haven't been out on the water in almost a year."

His smile was instantaneous. "Great, I'll pick you up around six."

She coughed. "In the morning?" She almost dropped her keys.

He chuckled. "Don't worry; you'll have plenty of sleep." He glanced down at his watch. "It's only a quarter to ten."

She frowned. "Yeah, but who says I'm going to bed now? Or soon for that matter. I'm not even tired." She sighed.

His smile grew. "Then let me in." He leaned closer. His hands went to her hips as he pulled her against his body. "I bet I can tire you out."

She felt his hard body next to hers and felt her own

body respond to the promise his made. She knew how good his body would feel in her hands. She'd seen him plenty of times, shirtless, in surf shorts, dripping wet with water. How many times had she dreamed of his body next to hers? Of his hands roaming over her. His mouth… She sighed and shook her head.

"Not tonight, big boy," she purred as she took a step back towards her door. She ran her eyes up and down his body slowly and gave him a look. "Besides, old Cole is showing."

"Soon." It came out as a whisper. "Soon, you'll want to invite me in." He leaned his hand on her door just behind her head.

She pressed her shoulders against the cool wood and for a moment allowed herself to imagine what it would be like if she invited him in. Then she felt behind her and slid her key into the lock and was thankful that she got it on the first try.

"Thanks again for walking me home." She started to turn.

"Wendy?" He waited until she turned back, then he leaned in slowly, giving her time to step back, but she held her ground. The kiss was slow and sweet with promises that she doubted he could keep. "I'll see you at six."

She nodded, fearing she couldn't find her voice. She stepped into her apartment and shut the door solidly behind her.

The fact that she had to lean against her closed door for almost two minutes to catch her breath and steady her heart did little to assure her that he was a bad idea.

Looking around her condo, she decided to spend the energy she felt bursting through her entire body by cleaning up the mess. She may want stability in her life, but her condo looked like a teenager lived there.

Why she found it so hard to keep the tiny place clean was beyond her. Maybe it was because she'd never had a good role model growing up or because she'd been running a house when she should have been going out with friends or playing sports in school.

She spent the next two hours cleaning, dusting, vacuuming, and even boxing up old items she no longer needed. She planned on delivering them to the local donation center later that week.

By the time she walked into her bathroom and started filling up her tub with hot water and bubbles, she felt sore and satisfied.

If Cole could try to turn over a new leaf, so could she. Starting now, her condo would not only be clean, but organized.

She couldn't stop herself from dreaming about Cole as she sunk lower in the sudsy water. Or from dreaming of how wonderful it had felt to be held, touched again. She knew it was going to be very difficult tomorrow to fight the attraction she had for him.

Sinking lower in the water, she tried to stop her body from remembering how wonderful it had felt to have his hands on her.

CHAPTER 3

Cole smiled over at Wendy as he leaned against the wheel of the small sailboat. The twenty-six-footer was nothing special, but it was still in great shape and, most important, didn't leak.

He and his brothers had been taking *Pete*, the name Marcus had given the old thing years ago, out on the water for as long as Cole could remember. Roman had taken the old guy in several years back and had redone the entire cabin. Now, instead of old mattresses and waterlogged cushions below deck, there was a small kitchen, a sitting area, and a state-of-the-art cabin with a queen-sized bed. There was even a flat-screen television down there.

He didn't know why his brother had fixed it up, but he and Marcus had no complaints about it. Now, even their aunt was taking it out on day trips.

"Do you go out often?" Wendy leaned against the railing as she sat back.

"Not as often as I want. I was born to be on the water."

He looked around and lifted his face towards the sun. When he heard her laugh, he glanced down at her.

"Anyone can see that. All they have to do is look at you." She smiled up at him.

"What about you?"

She looked at him, her eyebrows shooting up in question.

"You said it's been a while since you've been out. What's kept you away."

She sighed. "Well, I broke up with Kevin. He had a thirty-two-foot Catalina." She sighed. "He used to take me out on the water every other weekend."

He frowned a little as he thought about getting a bigger boat. "Why did you ditch the guy then?"

She chuckled and looked up at him. Her eyes were half hidden under the cap she wore. Her long blonde hair was tied back from her face. He could see that her cheeks had already turned a light shade of pink from the wind. "Because it wasn't all about how big his boat was..."

He blinked a few times and felt his own face flush as desire spread through him quickly. His fingers flexed a few times on the wheel as he tried to rein in his lust for her. What he wanted to do was throw the anchor overboard and haul her downstairs to take her as many ways as he could. He couldn't answer her since he didn't know how to reply. Plus, he didn't trust himself to keep the old Cole in check like he'd promised her.

"Are you going to let me steer?" She smiled up at him when he was silent. Since his mind was already in the gutter, images of her straddling him flooded it.

She chuckled. "Move over." She nudged him with her hip until he stepped aside. He sat along the railing and leaned back to watch her. There was a smile on her lips as she steered them out of the bay and into the clear waters of the gulf.

"So, what's between you and Alan?" he blurted out.

She glanced at him and frowned slightly. "What do you mean?"

He shrugged his shoulders. "Rose mentioned something about the two of you…" He waited and watched as recognition crossed her eyes. Then she smiled.

"Jealous?"

He stopped his chin from dropping and chose to shrug his shoulders and remain silent.

She smiled and continued to steer them away from the crowded beaches.

"Well?" he said a few minutes later when he couldn't stand her silence.

She looked over at him and smiled. He could tell she believed she'd won a little war. "Alan is a good friend. I've known him since I took my first job back in high school."

"And?"

She shrugged his shoulders. "I was happy when he came back from his tour in the Marines in one piece. He's the reason I tend bar. He taught me everything I know."

"And now you're his boss."

She smiled. "It's not that he thinks of me as his boss so much as he just doesn't want to be a boss, so it doesn't matter to him that I'm higher than him."

"Oh?" He crossed his ankle over his knee and watched her closely.

She shook her head. "He had a rough time shortly after he came back. He likes the low commitment. Being a supervisor doesn't fit well with what he wants in life right now."

"What do you want?"

The question seemed to surprise her. She blinked a few times and looked off to where a school of dolphins played off the port side of the boat.

He watched sadness flood her eyes, then she sighed. "I'm still working on that."

He stood up and walked over to her, resting his hands over hers on the large wheel. "There's plenty of time."

She glanced over her shoulder at him. "Easy for you to say. You've always known what you wanted."

"Yeah, but getting it is a different story." His eyes bore into hers. He loved the way her eyes heated when she understood his meaning.

He didn't know what had caused him to say it, but it was the truth. He did know what he wanted, at least for now. Her. But convincing her that he was a good idea was turning out to be more difficult than he'd expected.

They sailed south along the coastline for almost an hour before he finally threw anchor at one of his favorite fishing spots.

"What do you say we catch some fish?" She smiled and nodded.

They sat on the back of the small boat for over an hour. When his stomach growled, he pulled some sandwiches his aunt had made for them from the cooler.

They caught and released over a dozen small fish before, finally, a larger one took the bait.

"You're going to let him get away," she warned, trying to take hold of his line with her gloved hand.

"No, I'm not." He chuckled and grabbed the belt on

her shorts since she was leaning over the side of the boat a little too far for his comfort.

"Reel him in," she commanded, trying to get the net under the massive fish. It was big enough that he actually had to grip the side of the railing to haul it up.

"Oh, isn't he beautiful," she exclaimed as the bright red fish flopped around in the net. He'd caught plenty of snapper in his life and they all looked the same to him.

"You think he's good looking now, wait until he's grilled up for dinner." He plopped the fish into the live hold. "Guess we'd better find him some friends if we plan on having enough for everyone."

"Everyone?" She glanced at him in question as she checked her fishing pole, which was sitting in its holder.

He chuckled as he baited his line and tossed it in the water again. "Sure. Dad, Aunt Julie, Marcus, and Shelly. Cassey and Luke had plans with his folks tonight."

She shook her head. "I just assumed…"

"What?" He slid his fishing pole into the holder and glanced over at her. He liked that fact that he could read her thoughts, which were clearly written in her eyes. "There's a lot you don't know about me." He sat next to her on the bench and watched her.

Sighing, she glanced out at the water. "It must have been wonderful growing up with your family."

He chuckled at how easily she could change a subject. "It did have its moments."

"You're all adopted, correct?" She glanced at him.

He nodded and felt a sense of pride, knowing that they all thought of each other as blood.

"Do you…" She stopped, and he watched her bite her bottom lip. He knew the question. He'd been asked it tons of times. By the media and by friends. He'd asked himself the same thing over and over.

"Do I ever think about my real folks?"

She nodded, and he reached over and took her hand. Enjoying the way her small fingers felt in his, he ran his thumb over her palm slowly.

"I've avoided telling the media, but my real parents were killed shortly after I turned eight." He turned his head and looked off over the water. He could still remember their faces and hear their laughter.

"I'm sorry." She looked down at their joined hands.

"I'd like to think that they would have approved of the Graytons." He smiled. "I mean, we all had such a wonderful time growing up together." He tugged on her hand. "What about you? You've told me about your old man and your stepmother, but I haven't heard about your real mom."

She frowned a little and he wondered if she had a story like his brothers or sisters did. Maybe he was digging too deep, too soon.

"I never knew her; she died giving birth to me. Dad took it hard and snapped, I guess. My mother was the love of his life, or so he always told me. When she died, I guess so did his stability and sanity."

"I'm sorry." He rubbed her hand in his, not knowing what more to say to her. He'd gotten a hint at why she acted the way she did around him last night. He wasn't entirely sure why, but it meant a lot to him to prove to her that he was nothing like her old man.

She sighed and leaned back, dropping his hand so she could rest back on her elbows. "You know, I always wanted siblings. When Willow came along, I thought it was my chance to finally have a normal family."

"Normal is boring," he admitted under his breath.

She chuckled. "You would think that. I mean, have you ever done anything normal in your life?"

Her eyes sparkled as she smiled at him. He laughed. "I did go to prom."

She chuckled. "Right."

"Course, I took three girls as my dates."

She sat up a little. "Did they know about each other?"

He nodded, remembering the fun night. "Two of them were even sisters."

She shook her head and sighed. He could tell a reprimand was coming so he tugged on her until she leaned against his side. "Not everything is as cut-and-dried as you think."

"Oh?" Her hands went to his chest as she tried to hold herself up.

Nodding, he continued. "I originally asked one sister, but she had asked a girlfriend who was home-schooled to go with her. You know, so the friend would get some sort of a prom experience." She nodded so he continued. "Well, since neither of them drove, and since her little sister hadn't been asked yet, she asked me if I would drive them all. So, technically I guess you could say I had three dates to prom."

She smiled and chuckled. "You must have been the most popular boy in school."

His smile faltered. "Actually, Roman was the prom king of our clan."

"Roman?" She thought about it a moment, then he watched her smile grow. "Fitting. He does have a way about him. Doesn't he?" She sighed and for a moment, he was a little jealous of his brother.

It was like high school all over again. His brother had never struggled with finding a date. The guy was freaking James Bond when it came to women falling over him. And they weren't like the women that came running to Cole, most of whom were just looking to spend a night or two with someone famous. No, Roman found the women that wanted long-term relationships, something Cole had spent his life trying to avoid. Then he looked over at Wendy and felt something shift deep inside him.

Feeling a little uncomfortable, Wendy sat next to Cole's father and watched Cole and his aunt argue over how to cook the fish they had caught that day. Not that there was any steam behind the argument, just humor. She'd never witnessed anything like it before and was glued to their every word.

Cole had even grabbed his aunt and had danced around the back porch trying to distract her from putting lemon pepper seasoning on the fillets.

"Cole Dalton Grayton." She dropped her hands to her hips and looked at him. Wendy could see a slight smile on the woman's lips. "The last time you tried to grill fish, they came out burnt."

"Maybe we should wait until Marcus gets here." He held the bottle of spices over his head, so his aunt couldn't reach it. Cole was a little over six foot, and his aunt was shorter than Wendy at five six. She was reaching and playfully jumping at Cole, trying to get the bottle from his reach.

She laughed. "I've made plenty of fish in my time, young man, and there is nothing wrong with the way I cook it." She stopped jumping and held out her hand.

Cole just looked at her and shook his head. "You're right. There is nothing wrong with your cooking," he said in a sarcastic voice with a smile.

Cole's father chuckled beside her, causing her to glance over at him.

Whispering, she leaned closer to the older man and asked, "What's this all about?"

He shook his head. "Every one of the boys fancies themselves the best chef." He smiled over at her and then said loud enough for everyone to hear, "Course, if my arthritis wasn't acting up, I'd get right over there and show them how it's done."

Smiling, Cole nodded. "Course you would, Pop." He'd dropped his guard long enough that his aunt had jumped up and grabbed the bottle from his hands.

"There!" Rushing over to the fish as she giggled, she dashed seasoning all over the fillets.

He groaned. "Really?" Just then there was a chuckle from behind them. She turned just in time to watch Marcus and Shelly walk up the back stairs.

"Lemon pepper again?"

Their aunt turned towards him with a frown and nodded her head. "Bout time you two got here. I thought I was going to have to cook all this myself." She smiled and walked over to hug the pair.

"If you'd been here five minutes earlier, you could

have helped me hide the bottle." Cole walked over and picked up the seasoning.

"What's up with the lemon pepper?" Wendy asked, leaning closer to their father.

Mr. Grayton smiled back at her. "Well, my Julie never really learned or had the patience to cook using anything but lemon pepper. It's sort of an addiction." He patted her hand. "Hope you like it. I know the boys outgrew it… oh, about two years after they came to us." He chuckled.

Marcus wrapped his arms around his aunt's shoulders and smiled down at her. "She would use it in everything, even macaroni, and cheese."

"Remember the time she made lemon pepper spaghetti." Cole cringed as he sat next to her.

She couldn't stop herself from laughing. Even when he wrapped his arm around her shoulders, her smile remained. She watched Shelly's eyebrows shoot up when she noticed Cole's move and decided she would have to talk to her friend alone, later.

"We caught 'em, you cook 'em." Cole nodded towards the fish when his brother tried to sit down across from them.

Marcus sighed. "While you two sat around on a boat and threw a couple lines in the water, I worked on the house all day. I'm not only beat, I'm sore as heck."

Laughing, Cole shook his head. "You know the rules."

Throwing his head back and groaning, Marcus walked over to the hot grill. "Fine, but I'm scraping this off and using different seasoning."

CHAPTER 4

By the time the food was served, Wendy was feeling more comfortable. She had a wonderful time talking with the group and had laughed as much as she always did around the Grayton family members.

Their aunt, Julie, was even funnier than Marcus. But what had really thrown her for a loop was their father, Mark. The man was not only sharp as a tack but was so quick on the comebacks that Wendy almost felt her head spin.

She could see where Marcus and Cole had gotten their wit. Cole took after his aunt so much, and she wondered if they noticed how alike they were.

The more time she spent with them, the more she liked them. When the food was gone, they sat around the small fire pit and talked. It was too warm to have a fire going, but that didn't stop the men from propping their feet up on the stone and leaning back in their chairs. It was clear someone had taken the time to make it cozy out here, and she could tell this was something the family did often. She liked knowing that someone had taken the time to make it so inviting.

Part of her was jealous of Cole and his family. She'd always dreamed of having what he had, but even so, she'd never imagined it could be like this.

When Marcus and Shelly left, Cole took her hand and pulled her up from her chair.

"We'd better head out too. Dad needs his rest." He nodded to where his father was starting to doze off in his chair. The man's feet were propped up, his arms were crossed over his chest, and a light snore was coming from his lips. When Cole spoke, however, his eyes opened.

"I'm not as young as I used to be," the older man said, shaking his head as he got up slowly from his chair.

"Liar, you were never young." Cole laughed as he helped the man up from his chair.

Laughing, Mr. Grayton slapped Cole on the shoulder. "Ain't that the truth." He shook his head. "Well, it was sure nice to finally meet you." He held out his hand to her.

She walked over and hugged the frail-looking man.

"Oh, well." She watched his face turn a little red. "You come back any time you want." He smiled and patted her arm.

She nodded as she felt a lump in her throat. "Thank you for having me." She shook Julie's hand. The woman wasn't having any of it and pulled her into her arms for a hug.

"If he gets one…" She smiled. "We always have a big party for July Fourth. We take the party boat to Crab Island and watch the fireworks. We'd love to have you along."

Wendy shook her head. "I… I'll have to check my schedule."

As Cole drove them back across the bay bridge, she sat and looked out the dark windows, thinking about the evening.

"You're awful quiet over there," he said as they hit the other side of the bay.

She sighed. "I was just thinking about your family."

"Good or bad?" He glanced over at her.

She smiled. "Good. I like them a lot."

He smiled and turned his eyes back to the road. "Good. They like you too."

"Like I said, it must have been wonderful growing up there."

He nodded. "I'm sure you had your moments too."

She closed her eyes and thought about it. "I suppose. But mostly I was on my own."

He reached over and took her hand in his. Her first instinct was to pull away, but it felt good, so she relaxed back and enjoyed the rest of the drive to her condo.

"So," he said as he pulled into her parking lot. "What are we doing tomorrow?"

She laughed. "I don't know what you're doing, but I was planning on hitting the mall and then the grocery store."

"Good, I'll pick you up around eleven."

She shook her head. "Cole."

"Oh, come on. I've got nothing better to do." He shut off the engine and turned towards her.

She looked at him for a moment. "Don't get me wrong, I've had a really nice day, but…"

He reached across the seat and quickly pulled her towards him. By the time he stopped, she was almost in his lap.

"Cole!" she said right before his lips took hers. She wanted to fight him off, but the second his mouth touched hers, she went lax. Actually, every muscle in her body went from tense to on fire. How was it that just the slight touch of his lips could turn her into a complete dolt?

Finally, when she was almost completely breathless, he leaned back and smiled at her. "You were saying…"

She shook her head and realized she'd totally forgotten what they had been talking about. Reaching over, she punched him on the arm quickly.

"Don't do that."

He chuckled and rubbed his shoulder. "You didn't seem to mind a minute ago."

She glared at him. "No!" She finally remembered their earlier conversation.

"No, you didn't mind?" His smile grew.

"No, I'm not taking you shopping with me tomorrow." She watched his eyes for any hint of disappointment; instead, she only found more determination. That was one of the main reasons he'd set her off so easily in the past few years. He was always so sure of himself.

She looked down and realized his hand was running over her hip so she scooted back over to her side of the car.

"Thanks again for today." She reached for her door, but he stopped her with a hand on her arm.

"Wendy, I didn't mean to sound overbearing."

She glanced at him and could see something cross his eyes. She sighed and dropped her hand. "I know. You just can't help it."

He chuckled. "I guess it's going to take a while for the old Cole to fade away."

She nodded. "Maybe you should try to take it in steps?" She smiled.

He chuckled. She had always loved the rich sound, not to mention the way his silver eyes sparkled when he laughed.

"Okay, I'll back off. But I'd really like to see you again. I don't know how long I'll be in town this time."

She frowned when she thought about some of the reasons he'd be leaving.

"I should be back around six." She sighed and hated that he could home in on her weakness.

"How about dinner?" he piped in.

She thought about it and nodded slowly. "Fine."

He flashed her a smile and then jumped out and rushed around to open her door for her.

"I guess it would be too much for you to ask me in?" He leaned closer to her as she got out of his car.

Then she looked up at him and laughed. "Good night, Cole." She ducked around him and made it to her door. When she looked back, he was leaning against the hood of his car, watching her.

"Night," he called out and waved as she stepped in and closed the door behind her.

Glancing over at her clock, she groaned. What was she going to do with herself? It was only half past nine and she was still wired. Even the early morning couldn't stop her internal clock from keeping her up until one or two.

Dropping her bag on the table, she walked over and picked up the remote and tried to keep her mind off the fact that she'd just had the best day of her life with a man she had promised to hate forever.

※

Cole slammed down his cell phone, only because he was afraid he'd throw it if he didn't get it out of his hands quickly. Pacing, his long legs ate up the tiny apartment.

Where the hell was he? He rolled his shoulders as he paced and thought about the last time he and his brother Roman had talked.

"You've got to cover for me," Roman said as he threw clothes into his bag.

"Why?" Cole had leaned against the doorjamb and watched his brother shove clothes in the small bag. The fact that his neat and tidy brother wasn't folding everything twice before placing it neatly into a large duffle bag had shocked him. But he'd stood back and watched the show.

"Just for a few weeks or so." Roman had turned on him. "If you don't, I'll tell Aunt Julie about the time you used her new ironing board to ride the 'waves' down the stairs."

Cole chuckled. "Bringing out the big guns, huh?"

Roman nodded. "When it's important."

Cole shrugged his shoulders. What was it to him if his brother wanted to disappear for a while? After all, Cole had been doing it on and off for the last few years himself.

"Fine, but at least tell me where you're going."

Roman stood up after zipping the large duffel bag and turned towards him. "I can't."

Cole stood up and uncrossed his arms. "Listen, you want to go off somewhere and do God-only-knows-what, that's fine with me. You want me to keep a secret from the family, that's okay too. But at least tell someone where you are. Just in case. That's rule number one, bro."

Roman had sighed and closed his eyes. "I'm not leaving the state." His brother's brown eyes found his. "That's all I can tell you."

Cole waited. "And?"

Roman shook his head, and Cole realized that his sandy blond hair was longer than normal. Actually, his normally clean-cut, shaved, and suited brother had been looking scruffy the last few days. Cole had noticed the change only a few days after he'd arrived back in town.

Cole had been on a shoot for a new line of cologne in Europe, and when he'd returned, the apartment had been a mess, and his brother had looked like he hadn't shaved in days. He'd actually been wearing a dirty T-shirt and shorts.

"Just tell everyone I had some business to tend to in Atlanta. They'll assume it has to do with Spring Haven."

Cole had sighed. "How long will you be gone?"

Roman shrugged his shoulders, something all three boys did the same, reminding them they were brothers.

"Fine, but I can't hold the fort down for too long. I've got a contest next month in Hawaii."

He nodded. "It shouldn't take that long." He turned and picked up his bag.

"Don't forget to take your phone." He tossed his brother his new cell phone, a device he'd never seen his brother leave home without. Actually, Roman was always glued to the damn thing; it was any wonder he didn't have it stapled to his ear.

Roman frowned down at it. "Right." He shoved it in the end of his bag and started to walk out.

"Check in every once in a while," Cole yelled at his brother's back as he walked out the front door. He thought he saw his head bob in reply but couldn't be sure since his hair was now longer than his own.

Cole walked over and glanced at his phone one more time. It had been over a week since Roman had disappeared and he'd yet to hear a single word from him. Every text, every voice mail of his had gone unanswered. He was beginning to wonder if he should tell the family.

He'd really hoped to go with Wendy today to Panama City. He was desperate for any distractions, even if it meant he'd have to go shopping with a girl.

He'd dated enough women in the last few years to know that when a woman went to the mall, she would usually walk out with handfuls of bags. He cringed inwardly at the memory of his last trip to a mall. Even that hadn't kept him from wanting to go with her today.

He'd been telling her the truth. He really did want to turn over a new leaf. In the last two years, he'd worked up a reputation as a womanizer in the media's eye. His agent had encouraged him to keep up the facade. Okay, most of it hadn't been for show. After all, when women—greatlooking women—fell at his feet, who was he to turn them away?

But after a while, he started realizing that no matter what he did, or who he dated, they were all the same: boring, shallow, and out for a piece of his fame.

Every time he brought a woman back home, they acted grateful for a short while, like it was all some sort of vacation. But after a few days or so, they would get bored and start complaining that he wasn't taking them out enough. That they weren't being *"seen"* together.

He wanted someone who actually liked being in Surf Breeze. After all, that's where he lived.

He frowned as he sat down on the sofa. His brother's sofa. Looking around the apartment, he realized that he didn't really live anywhere.

When he was in town, he'd always just stay at Roman's. Up until a few months ago, Marcus had lived in the small two-bedroom place as well. Cole used to just take the sofa or, if he had a lady, stay at a hotel not far from there.

But now that Marcus and Shelly had bought a place and were fixing it up, the second room of Roman's place was all his. He shot money his brother's way to help pay for the rent, along with his share of keeping Spring Haven Home, the boy's home he and Roman had started, running. All of them pitched in to keep the place going.

He was really proud of them for stepping out and helping young kids that were in the same situation that they had been in growing up. He knew that the home ate up a lot of Roman's time, even though he had a staff of people helping to run the place. Roman spent most of his time across the bay in Spring Haven while Marcus spent most of his time with their other business, Paradise Construction.

He and his siblings had each chosen their own paths. He frowned thinking about it. He had always known what he wanted to do. Surf. He hadn't expected to make so much money at it or to become a celebrity. But when his agent had approached him a few years back about modeling underwear, he'd needed the dough to pay for his bike, so he'd jumped at the chance. He'd never imagined that he would slingshot into stardom overnight.

Now his face and his body were on more billboards than most movie stars. He'd continued to win prestigious surfing awards, which had only boosted the demand for his photo even more. Now, he spent more time traveling for photo shoots than he did on the water.

He crossed his arms over his chest and propped his feet up on the coffee table. Maybe that's why he was feeling antsy lately. Something had to give.

His mind switched gears to Wendy. It had been months since he'd had any desire to go out with anyone. At first, he'd thought that it was just because he was busy, but after a while, he'd figured out that he'd actually been turning women down when they approached him.

Maybe he'd head over to Cassey's and see if anything was going on. Better yet, he'd take the paddle board out on the water. He glanced at the window and smiled when he saw sun streaming through it.

Jumping up from the sofa, he rushed to the door and got everything together. He was just pulling away from the apartment parking lot when his phone chimed. Pulling over, he looked down and sighed when he saw his brother's face pop onto his screen.

"Hey." He glanced in the mirror to make sure he was all the way off the road.

"Hey, tell me you're around somewhere close." He could hear the pleading in his brother's voice.

"Umm." He closed his eyes and knew that his time chilling in the water wasn't going to happen. "I'm about half a mile from your driveway. Why?"

Marcus sighed. "Perfect. I could use another pair of hands for a while." He sighed. "I've got beer and pizza," he jumped in before Cole could answer.

"I'll be there in a few. I've got to head back and change into work clothes."

"Thanks, you're a real—" Cole heard a loud bang. "Gotta go." His brother hung up quickly.

Cole flipped his old truck around and went back to change into old jeans, a T-shirt, and his brown work boots. He'd dropped one too many things on his feet in the past helping his brothers out to show up at a job site without steel-toed boots.

When he arrived at Marcus and Shelly's new place, he knew he was in for a long day. There was a large cement truck blocking the driveway, so he had to park on the side of the street. There were five guys working on pouring the new driveway as he made his way up to the house.

Marcus swung open the door before he even had a chance to knock.

"Bout time." His brother was already covered in a layer of white dust. "We're in the bedroom dry-walling today." He turned and started walking towards the back of the house. Cole shut the door and followed him. "Sure sucks that Roman is out of town. We could have used his help today too."

When they walked into the master bedroom, Cole tried not to groan. He'd forgotten there were vaulted ceilings in the room and when he noticed there was scaffolding, he wished Roman was there too. Even when he saw Luke leaning against a large piece of drywall, holding it in place, he didn't feel better. Not that Luke wasn't a hard worker. But Marcus and Roman had an unspoken system when they worked together. It was spooky at times how the two of them could read each other's minds and finish a job quickly.

"When did you say that SOB was coming back?" Marcus walked over and quickly screwed in the drywall piece that Luke had been holding.

"Didn't." Cole walked over and positioned the next piece for Marcus.

Marcus glanced at him. "Don't think I don't know you're hiding something about that whole deal." His eyes narrowed. "But I'm too busy to hound you right now."

Cole nodded, silently cursing Roman again as he held up the piece of drywall, so Marcus could secure it.

CHAPTER 5

Wendy loved shopping. Period. There was no downside to it. She loved spending her hard-earned money on items she could enjoy, whether it was clothing or items for her condo. She loved picking things out and had a knack for getting what she wanted at a bargain.

Her sister and friends had always made fun of how much she'd spent when she was younger. It was hard to explain to them that it was her one reprieve from being so damn responsible all the time. But even in this, she was still sensible. She had one, and only one, a credit card that she allowed herself to spend out of. She paid it off each month and never maxed it out.

Sighing, she glanced down at the plum dress shoes and knew that her shopping budget wouldn't allow for them this month. That didn't stop her from admiring them as she walked around and glanced at every mirror in the shoe department.

She'd already picked out two pairs of shoes from the

sales rack that she was determined to get, a pair of sexy silver heels that went with the new skirt she'd bought at the last store and a pair of sensible low black boots she could easily wear at work.

She stopped off at the food court around lunchtime and had a bowl of noodles and chicken from her favorite Chinese place. Then, since she was feeling a little down about not being able to spend the weekend with her sister, she topped her lunch off with a cinnamon roll from the pretzel place.

She spent the rest of her time in the container store, buying things for her condo that would help her become better organized. She was determined to turn over a new leaf. After all, if Cole was so determined to try, why couldn't she? She viewed it as a challenge, and she was determined to win.

She finished off her day of shopping with a quick run into the grocery store. She hated grocery shopping. She always ate out instead of cooking. She blamed it on her work hours, but the truth was she hated cooking for just herself.

When Willow was younger, she'd enjoyed planning out meals and trying new ideas, and she'd loved to sit down around the table and eat. But since she was only cooking for one, she found herself grabbing food on the run, more and more.

When she drove up to her condo, she frowned when she saw Cole sitting on her small front patio. His long legs were stretched out, resting on the railing as he leaned back in her rocking chair. When she got a little closer, she realized he was wearing long, faded jeans with holes in them and a dirty T-shirt that had seen better days. His tan arms were crossed over his chest, showing off those sexy muscles she'd always admired. He was even wearing work boots, which were crossed over each other.

She stopped dead in her tracks with two large bags of groceries in her arms when she heard him snoring. Her eyes zeroed in on his face to confirm that he was dead asleep. His mouth was slightly opened. She was thankful there wasn't any drool coming out of it. Chuckling to herself, her eyes moved over the rest of him.

You know, with his eyes closed like this, he looked rather harmless. Until she found herself looking at those lips. Why, oh, why couldn't she stop thinking about that kiss last night or the ones from before?

She wet her lips and all of a sudden felt the warmth of the evening creeping into every pore of her body. She didn't know how long she stood there, but when she realized the snoring sounds had stopped, her eyes flew to his. Had she ever realized just how silver blue they were?

"Hey." He smiled up at her as he stretched. "Sorry. I guess my brother worked me harder than I thought today." She watched how his arms went over his head as he rolled his neck a few times. "Man, hanging drywall sure takes a lot out of you."

She nodded, not really sure what he was saying. Her mouth had gone completely dry watching his slow movements.

"So…" He stood up and took the heaviest bag from her hands then peeked inside. "What's for dinner?"

She chuckled and moved around him. "You just show up here, expecting dinner?"

"No." He followed her into her condo and set the bag

he'd been carrying down next to hers. "How about a shower and dinner?" He looked down at himself.

She laughed. She couldn't help it. He'd shaken his hair and a plume of dust had fallen all over her counter.

"Go." She pointed to her bathroom. "Don't make a mess." She started pulling items out of the bags so she could put together a dinner, but before she got far, she was being turned around and Cole's lips were on hers. This kiss was fast and potent, and then he was walking into her bathroom, whistling what sounded like a Beach Boys' song.

How the hell was she supposed to fight against an attraction that strong? Especially when her body was so easily betraying her. It took almost an entire minute, leaning against the counter and breathing slowly, for her heart rate to get back to normal. Then she turned her mind to the simple and enjoyable task of cooking for two.

Cole stood under the hot water and let it roll down his back. Every muscle in his body hurt, but it was his hip that was causing most of the throbbing. Glancing down at it, he sighed when he noticed the large red splotches crossing his skin.

After standing under the spray for a while, he pulled himself from Wendy's small shower and dried off. He hunted through her medicine cabinet and swallowed a few aspirins before donning his clothes again. He'd shaken them out, but he wished he'd swung by his place before coming over here.

It had been a knee-jerk reaction to drive to her place after he'd left Marcus's house. He'd wanted to see her, plain and simple. He hadn't expected to fall asleep waiting for her to get home, or that his hip would have stiffened to the point it had. But when he'd caught her looking at him on her front porch, it had all been worth it.

She couldn't deny the heat and desire he'd seen in her blue eyes. He was sure it had matched his own desire for her, especially when he'd seen her lick her lips. It had taken all his willpower not to let the old Cole out and haul her into her place and take her hard and fast.

He sighed and glanced at himself in the foggy mirror. He needed another damn haircut. Shaking his head, he watched his blond hair curl up and smiled. Well, maybe it could hold off for another week.

When he opened the bathroom door, the wonderful smells of home cooking hit him, and he forgot all about his hip and focused on his stomach instead.

"Something smells good," he said, walking up behind Wendy as she stood at the stove. His hands went to her hips and he moved close enough to feel her body next to his.

"I hope you like manicotti." She sighed as he ran his mouth over the column of her neck. He felt her lean back a little towards him.

"Hmmm," he moaned against her skin, "love it."

"Cole, dinner is going to burn if you keep doing that." She giggled.

He nodded. "Okay." Her skin tasted so good, he just had to have one more nibble.

"Why don't you grab us both a beer." She sighed.

He nodded again, his lips hovering over the softness behind her ear. "Kay."

She giggled and then turned and pushed him away.

"Beer. Now." She smiled at him until his eyes focused again.

"All right." He chuckled and walked over to her fridge. After popping the top on two beers, he leaned against the counter and watched her move.

He'd always been impressed by how she bartended. It was like watching a dancer behind the bar. He especially enjoyed it when there was a live band playing; he loved watching her hips move to the music. Glancing around now, he spotted her radio and walked over to find some music she could sway to as she cooked. It took some doing, but finally, he found a good station and was rewarded almost instantly as she moved around the kitchen, hips pumping as she went.

"How did you get into bartending?"

She reached over and took a deep sip of her own beer.

She glanced back at him and smiled. "It was either that or stripping." She chuckled when his chin dropped.

"Seriously?" He felt his mouth go dry as a million images rushed through his mind.

"Sure, I needed a lot of money and had no skills."

"What stopped you?" He took a long drink of his beer to cool his libido down.

She shrugged her shoulders and turned back towards the stove. "I was fifteen at the time and looked it, so I started waiting tables instead."

He blinked. "You started working at fifteen?"

She nodded again. "With a kid sister to take care of… Remember?"

He nodded. "I just thought…" He shook his head and mentally cursed her father.

"What?" She turned back towards him as she leaned on the counter.

He sighed. "You said something about your dad sending money."

She laughed. "Sure, I'd get an envelope with a few hundred bucks every month. It helped pay for the rent and nothing else. There were the electric and water bills, not to mention keeping food on the table."

He crossed his arms over his chest and frowned when he realized he had never had to worry about anything like that. Not once in his life. Even after his folks had died, he'd been rushed to the Grayton's and his nonchalant lifestyle had continued.

"What about school?"

She shrugged her shoulders. "I went until it got in the way of work, then I went in and got my GED." She shrugged and then bent down and pulled a steaming hot pan from the oven.

"Your sister?" he asked.

She glanced up at him and shook her head. "I made her finish school."

"What about college?"

She smiled. "Willow is going to FSU."

He smiled along with her. "That's great."

She nodded and then frowned a little. "Course, if her grades keep dropping, I'm seriously thinking about having her finance her own way next semester."

He was sure his chin dropped. "You… You're paying for your sister's college?"

She frowned at him. "Who else is going to do it?"

He shook his head. "What about grants? Scholarships?"

She nodded. "We applied for a lot, got some. They helped for a while."

"But?"

She sighed. "Ever since Willow's new boyfriend, her grades have dropped too low to maintain them."

"Have you talked to her?" He set his beer down and walked over to take her shoulders in his hands. When her eyes went back to his, he could see the sadness in them.

"I was going to… this weekend." She shook her head and he saw her eyes light up again. "What about you?"

"Me?"

"Sure, why didn't you get some school under your belt?" She took a step back. "Too busy jet-setting around the world?" She chuckled as she set a pot aside.

"I guess I never really thought about it."

She glanced back at him. "Why not? I mean, I know surfing was your dream, but surely you want something else… after."

The word hung in the air. After. He'd never really thought about after his surfing career was over. Would it end? Why? Only one reason came into his mind and he shook the thoughts from his head.

"No, I guess I've never really thought about it."

"What was your backup plan? I mean, growing up, didn't you want to be something else too?"

He smiled. "Nothing as sexy as a stripper."

She laughed. "I saw the last ad you were in. You might as well be a stripper with as few clothes as you were wearing."

He chuckled. "Touché." He walked over and pulled her close and then his lips were on hers as his hands held her still.

"Now I've had dessert before dinner." He smiled down at her as he pulled back.

They sat at her little table and ate some of the best manicotti he'd ever had, including the manicotti he'd had on the trip to Italy he'd taken last summer. They talked about her sister and his family for a while. She seemed very curious about Marissa, his sister who had run away at seventeen.

"So, Cassey doesn't talk about her a lot, but I get the feeling every one of you is hurt by her sudden disappearance." She leaned forward a little and moved her empty plate aside.

He nodded and scooped up another healthy helping for himself. "Yeah, all of us took it hard. Especially Pop." He shook his head. "He'd helped turn around five of us, and he couldn't help feeling a little like he'd failed us." He shook his head and shoved food into his mouth.

"Why? I mean, from what I've seen, the four of you are pretty great."

He smiled. "Thanks."

She sighed and tilted her head a little. "You know what I mean."

He nodded, and then his smile fell away a little. "Marissa was just like us. I mean, we all thought so. She was our sister. At least she acted like it."

"You don't think…" She left the unspoken question hanging in the quiet room.

He knew what she was hinting at, and had thought it a million times himself, but quickly shook his head no.

"No, the police say she ran away. She left a note for Cass."

Wendy nodded. "That's good. I mean…" She shook her head.

"I know, it's better that she ran away than the alternative. We've all thought that for years now."

She sighed and leaned back in her chair as she sipped her second beer. "Any thoughts as to why she left?"

He finished off his third helping and pushed his plate aside. "I have a few." He sipped his beer and leaned back, crossing his arms over his chest.

"And?" She leaned forward a little.

He sighed. "Her mother came to see her shortly before she ran away."

Wendy's eyebrows shot up. "I thought… you were all orphans."

He shook his head no. "Marcus's mother, Roman's folks, and Marissa's mother are all still alive."

She nodded, and he could see her mind working, full of questions.

"Their stories aren't mine to tell. Marissa had mentioned something to Cass the night before about ending up like her mother." He shook his head in disgust. "Let's just say there was no possibility of that, ever."

"Did the police check with her after your sister went missing?"

He nodded. "She just laughed and said she'd ended up like her after all."

"What does that mean?"

He shrugged his shoulders. "Apparently she'd run away from home when she was young."

"Has anyone heard from her? I mean, how long has it been?"

"Almost eight years now. Each of us has taken turns

looking for her. Roman thought he saw her at the hospital when I had my bike accident."

"Really?" Her eyes lit up.

"Yeah, but he's had a few other close calls like that. I swear each and every one of us scans every crowd looking for her."

"What does she look like?" she asked, leaning her chin on her hand.

"Here." He pulled out his cell phone and flipped through the images, inwardly cringing at all the women he had pictures of on the damned thing. First thing in the morning, he was wiping his phone memory. "This is all of us the summer before she left." He smiled down at the picture of everyone standing on the small sailboat, and then he handed the phone to Wendy.

She held it close and scanned the image.

"That's her between Cass and Roman." He leaned closer and pointed to the screen. His eyes roamed over the image again.

"Is this your mother? Mrs. Grayton?" She pointed to the larger woman off to the side.

He nodded. "She died that winter." He felt the same sting behind his eyes as he always did when he thought of Elizabeth Grayton, his second mother. "Cancer," he said, still hating the taste of the word in his mouth.

She nodded. "No one should have to go through that." She sighed. "Even my father didn't deserve to."

He sighed. "I don't know about that. Leaving two young girls to fend for themselves." He shook his head.

"It had its moments." She smiled up at him. "I never had a bedtime, I was never nagged to brush my teeth." She smiled. "Look, they're still all there. Never a cavity." She chuckled.

"It must have been lonely." He reached across the table and took her hand.

She sighed. "There were times." She reached for her beer with her free hand. "I guess that's why I like bartending so much." Her smile was weak, but he could tell she really believed it. "Some nights, when I felt that way, I'd come back from work and..." she shrugged her shoulders. "I wasn't lonely. I guess I'm to blame for the rift between Willow and myself. I mean, I wasn't around a lot."

He squeezed her hand gently. "Still, she should have chosen hanging out with her sister over a boyfriend."

She giggled. "Would you have?"

He frowned and thought about it. "Hanging with Cass or Marissa verses hanging out with you?" He shook his head. "I suppose not."

She frowned. "I'm not..." She stopped herself and sighed as he smiled at her. "You are so frustrating."

He laughed. "Good. Now, I'll help you clean up, so we can sit on your sofa and make out like a couple of teenagers."

CHAPTER 6

*S*he tried not to let her nerves show, but she couldn't stop her hands from shaking as he moved closer to her. It had been nice standing beside him as he helped her clean up after dinner. She'd never had anyone help her in the kitchen before. Kevin hadn't been big on cleaning, nor had any other guy she'd been with before. She supposed it was the way Cole had been raised that gave him an underlying gentlemanly quality about him.

He opened doors, carried heavy items, cleaned, and was always so damn polite. She glanced out of the corner of her eye at him. He was watching the television like he was completely glued to it, but she knew better since his hand was resting on her shoulder.

She'd been itching to have him kiss her again just so the tension between them would stop. He'd hinted that he considered her his girlfriend and her heart had jumped out of her chest.

She wasn't sure about him yet. She'd known him

longer than any other guy she'd been involved with, but that didn't stop her from having her doubts about him. After all, she knew his history. She'd seen him wrapped up in bandages because he'd been a little too reckless.

She couldn't imagine what life would be like with someone like him. He would be jet-setting off around the world, living on the edge of death all the time, while she stayed home and worried. Not to mention the fact that he didn't have any ambitions outside of surfing and being a beach bum.

Sure, he had an awesome family. Okay, probably the best family she'd ever seen. But she wasn't dating his family.

Her breath hitched when she played those words over in her mind. Dating. Was she really thinking about getting into a relationship with Cole Grayton?

She glanced at him again as he leaned closer to her, and his arm tightened around her shoulders. "What?" He leaned closer.

"Hmm?" She turned her eyes back to the screen as he chuckled.

"You keep stealing glances." His finger went under her chin as he turned her head towards his. "What are you thinking about? Because obviously, you're not really into this show." He nodded towards the television.

She sighed and glanced at his lips and decided she didn't want to make up her mind about Cole just yet. Not until she'd had some fun. Who could blame her? It had been months since she'd had any fun. "You did mention something about making out like teenagers."

He smiled and tugged on her until she was almost in

his lap. "So, does this mean you've made up your mind to go out with me?" he said, a breath away from her lips.

"I…" She wet her lips in anticipation. "I haven't made up my mind yet." Her eyes went to his lips, waiting. She watched the sides of his mouth go up in a slight smile.

"What can I do to persuade you?" he said, before gently running his lips over hers. She couldn't stop the moan from escaping, not after she felt her entire body relax into his.

"You make it so hard for me to think." She smiled against his skin.

"Good, you've been doing too much of it anyway." His mouth traveled down her neck, sending bumps all over her body. Her fingers dug into his thick hair, holding him close to her body. Her eyes rolled to the back as his mouth found a spot she hadn't known could cause her to rush to the edge of orgasm so quickly.

"You like that?" He chuckled and then used his mouth on her again.

She knew she was probably making all sorts of crazy sounds, but when he kissed her collarbone, it drove her crazy. His fingers pushed her shirt aside, exposing more of her skin for his mouth to explore as her nails dug into his shoulders.

She rested her head back on the soft cushions and enjoyed his slow exploration. When his mouth left her skin, she moaned a little and then watched as he gently pushed her until she lay down on the sofa. She couldn't take her eyes off his fingers as they moved below her shirt, pushing it up until her entire belly was exposed.

"So soft." His eyes were glued to her stomach, roaming over her shorts and legs. "So pretty." She watched as his blond head dipped down and when his mouth touched her belly, she moaned and held on.

She felt his hands on her hips as he kissed his way across every inch of her exposed skin. When a finger dipped below her shorts, she almost jumped off the cushions with excitement.

"Easy." He chuckled. "We have time." His finger lazily dipped again, causing her skin to heat.

"Cole," she whimpered.

"I've got you." His hands moved to tug down her shorts, but the drawstring was tied and he spent some time slowly undoing it. When she was finally freed, he tugged on her cotton shorts until she lay before him in only white silk panties.

"Perfect," he cooed as he ran one finger down her hip. She watched as he dipped his mouth towards her skin and then sighed as his lips touched her silk-covered sex. His mouth was warm and wet on her and she felt herself building faster.

"Please," she begged. Her fingers dug into his hair as she spread her legs wider. When his finger dipped below her panties, she almost came undone. It had been too long. Too long since she'd enjoyed herself.

He finally pulled her panties aside, but his mouth just hovered over her. His eyes met hers and she saw him smile, and then he lowered his lips to her heated skin. She couldn't stop herself from crying out his name when her body convulsed in his hands.

Cole was blown away at Wendy's reaction. He'd never

witnessed anything so beautiful in his entire life. He'd heard the saying that women glowed with beauty but had never experienced it firsthand.

He wished he had a camera to capture the moment. Her long blonde hair was fanned out on the sofa cushions, and her shirt was bunched up around her gorgeous chest, exposing her flat, tan stomach. Her white silk panties were soaked from his mouth and her excitement, only making him harder than before. He could see her chest moving quickly with each breath and couldn't wait to see what she looked like after he'd made love to her.

Her eyes opened, and he watched her frown a little.

"Cole?" She reached for him only to have him shake his head.

"We have time." He slowly pulled her shorts back up her long legs, enjoying the silkiness of them as he went. "I bet you didn't know that I'm an ass man." He smiled up at her. She was still frowning at him and he almost laughed when she looked shocked.

"No, most men…" She broke off and shook her head as she tugged her shirt back into place.

He laughed. "Yeah, I've seen them stare at you. Not that I don't appreciate…" His eyes went to her ample chest. "But, this…" He let his hands slide over her hips then down farther to her ass and groaned.

She chuckled. "It's good to know I'm not lacking in that area."

He smiled and nodded as he helped her sit up. "I'd better get going." He stifled a yawn. "My brother is an ass to work for and I'm beat."

He watched her lips form an O. Her eyes went to his shorts and he felt like laughing again.

"Honey, I'd love to stay, but I'm afraid I couldn't give you all the attention you deserve. Not after the day, I put in." He pulled her close and kissed her for a while. "Trust me, I'd rather be taking you back to your bed than driving a few miles and crawling into an empty one."

She nodded and then chuckled when he yawned again. "You could stay…"

He rested his forehead on hers. "Tell me that again some other time."

She smiled and then got up. When he moved to get off the sofa, his hip chose that moment to spasm, so he fell backward and landed on the cushions with a groan.

"Are you okay?" She rushed back down to him, a frown on her face.

He nodded and closed his eyes for a moment, taking several deep breaths. He really was beat; every muscle in his body was screaming at him. He wanted to get back and swallow a few pills and clock out for the night. "Yeah, I guess I'm not used to a full day of hard labor." He smiled back at her and stretched his legs for show.

She chuckled and helped him up. "You should really think about doing yoga. It helps loosen your body. I can show you a few moves if you want."

He laughed. "Me? Doing yoga?" He shook his head as he laughed. Wendy put her hands on her hips and scowled at him.

"Suit yourself." She shrugged her shoulders. "You know; it could help out with your surfing."

He laughed harder. "Right. That sounds like something my brothers would say, right before I became the butt of a long string of jokes."

Wendy smiled at him. "I happen to know that Shelly

has convinced Marcus to go with her to yoga classes. They hold them above Ray's place." She sighed and rolled her eyes. "But, if your brother is a bigger man than you…"

He chuckled. "Nice try. If Marcus is doing yoga, I'll…" He shook his head.

"You'll what? Do it, too? You might be surprised. It could help." She nodded towards his hip. "Don't think you've fooled everyone, because ever since your accident, I've noticed your limp."

He frowned. "What do you mean?" He crossed his arms over his chest and waited.

She sighed. "I bet you didn't even go to physical therapy like you were supposed to."

He shrugged his shoulders. "I've been busy."

"Right." She laughed. "What was the last one's name?" She chuckled.

"Wendy." He smiled and pulled her close as she frowned.

"Don't remind me."

He leaned down and kissed her before she could disappear into her thoughts again. He didn't want to give her a moment to doubt starting a relationship with him. Now that he'd had a taste of her, he wanted to make sure he didn't lose her.

"Dream of me," he whispered against her lips. "When you crawl into bed, remember how this feels." He closed his lips over hers until he felt her shiver with want. Then he backed away slowly and left, leaving her standing in the middle of the room, her lips swollen from his.

When he got back to the apartment, the first thing he did was swallow a few pills and suck it all down with a cold beer. Then he made his way into the shower and stood under the hottest water he could stand on his skin. By the time he stepped out, his muscles were relaxed, and he felt almost human.

That was until he heard the message from Roman.

"Hey man, it's me. Um, I don't know how to tell you this, but I've found her. Marissa, that is. I'm staying longer. I don't know when I'll be back. Keep covering for me, will you? Oh, don't tell the family. Not yet. I'll be in touch."

That was it. The line went dead. Roman's voice had sounded off. Instantly, he picked up his phone and shot a text off to his brother.

-What the heck? You'd better call me back.

He waited a few minutes and then sent another.

-I'm not covering for you too much longer. I want answers. Is she okay?

Finally, ten minutes later, as he was crawling into bed, he heard his phone beep.

-She's fine. I'll tell you more later. Pls just cover for me.

-Okay. Where are you?

-later. Night.

Cole slammed his phone down before he threw it. How was he supposed keep covering for him? Already that day Marcus had cornered him and demanded to know what was up. Thankfully, the day had been so busy, he'd been able to avoid answering.

He knew he wasn't going to be as lucky next time and dreaded having to explain that Roman had gone off and found Marissa and kept it a secret from everyone else.

CHAPTER 7

The next day Wendy was back at work and loving every minute of it. Monday mornings were usually slower, but since it was the weekend before July Fourth, and they had a week full of live bands playing, the place was jammed.

She loved it when The Whalers, a local band who'd been playing at the bar and grill since opening, played. Mike, the guitar player, and singer had tried many times to get her to go out with him, but she just couldn't get past the fact that he was stuck in the 80s. Besides, he just wasn't her type. No, her type seemed to be blond, bad-boy surfers who had a knack for pissing her off. She glanced at the doorway and frowned when he walked in with Shelly on his arm. She knew that Shelly was completely devoted to Marcus, but the least Cole could do was not flirt with her so much.

She turned her eyes back to the beer she'd been building and scowled when it flowed over, soaking her hand in the process.

"Got something, or should I say, someone, on your mind tonight?" Alan chuckled behind her back.

"No! Shut up!" she whispered as she slid the drink across the bar and took the next order. She lived for busy nights and had a knack for always getting her orders right. No matter how many people were standing on the other side of the bar, she kept track of each and every one. Tonight, wasn't going to even be a challenge, but it was still fun in her book.

"Hey," she heard Cole's voice behind her. She turned to smile at the pair.

"Hi." She made a point to look towards the door. "Missing someone?"

Shelly laughed and hung her arm over Cole's shoulders, causing a little shiver of jealousy to rush down Wendy's spine. "Marcus will be along shortly. Cole was nice enough to walk me over."

She nodded, not trusting her voice. "What'll you have?" It wasn't that she didn't trust Shelly; it was more like she didn't trust Cole with Shelly.

"Club soda. I think I got food poisoning at lunch." She rubbed her stomach. "That's the last time I let Marcus convince me to try something new." She rolled her eyes. "FYI don't try the new Thai place at the edge of town."

"Noted." She handed over the club soda and looked at Cole, who was just staring at her.

"You?"

"Hmm?" He smiled at her.

"What'll you have?"

His smile grew bigger. "You know what I want."

She actually felt her cheeks turn pink, so she quickly turned around and started making the girlie drink that he liked. When she was done, she hoped her face had gone back to normal as she set the drink down in front of him.

His hand reached out and took hers, holding her still. When her eyes met his, she couldn't stop the smile from spreading on her lips.

"What?" She chuckled.

"Later?" She knew what he meant and even though Shelly was standing right next to him, she nodded quickly before pulling her hand away and taking the next order.

She didn't notice her feet or back hurting, not when she was enjoying the music so much. Her hips bounced along to the good tunes and she even stopped a few times to shake her booty during a favorite song.

Marcus showed up less than fifteen minutes later and the three of them made their way to their favorite booth near the back. She found it hard not to glance that way all night. Cassey had made her rounds and headed towards the booth. She knew her boss would be on her feet as much as anyone else in the place, which made her respect her even more.

She'd worked for plenty of people before, but none she'd liked as much as Cassey.

"Hey, baby, can I get a beer here?" When she turned around, she almost groaned out loud. Brad, one of the locals, was leaning on the bar with two of his buddies. Brad, Mark, and Joseph were Surf Breeze's local troublemakers. The three men caused more trouble in a season than most tourists did all year.

"What'll you have?" She prayed that they would have a beer each and then leave, but when he tossed down his credit card and opened a tab, she knew it was going to be a long night.

Sure enough, less than an hour later, right as the band decided to take a break, a small fight broke out between the trio and another group of men who had just walked in. Brad said that the newcomers had stolen a bar stool, which had caused Joseph to fall directly on his butt. But Wendy had been looking that way and had seen that Joseph had moved the stool aside to tell a story and had just been too drunk to remember.

It took Tyrone, a bouncer that worked on busy nights at the bar, along with Mike, two other band members, and both Marcus and Cole to clear the group out of the bar area. She was at least thankful that the cops hadn't been called. When they got involved, it usually shut the place down for a while.

After that, Cole took up residence at the bar instead of heading back to the booth.

"Does that happen a lot?" He frowned towards the doors.

She shrugged her shoulders. "The three of them usually only come in once a month. We've made it clear to them we're not going to deal with it."

He nodded and then looked back towards her. "I guess I never really thought about this place as a *bar* bar before."

She laughed as she started building a Guinness. "What did you think I do back here?"

He smiled and nodded. "You know what I mean."

She slid the Guinness across the bar to its owner. "Yeah, like I said, it doesn't happen often." She turned and took the next order and was happy to note that things were slowing down. The band was packing up and with no music to distract her, she was feeling every bit of pain from standing on her feet for the last eight hours.

"Does it bother you? Standing so long?" He leaned over the bar and snatched a handful of cherries from behind the bar.

She shrugged her shoulders and slapped at his hand. "Not so much. I like my job too much to care." She started cleaning up and closing down the bar. When she glanced at the clock, she smiled when she noticed that it was only a few minutes to one.

"But, your feet have to be killing you," Cole said, shoving a handful of cherries into his mouth.

She glanced at him and shook her head. "I'm sure there's still something in the kitchen to eat."

He shrugged his shoulders. "I'll have whatever you're having."

She rolled her eyes at him and placed her dinner order of cheese sticks and a turkey sandwich. Just for him, she added another sandwich and a side of chips and salsa and then made it all to-go instead of dine-in like she normally did.

"You were going to tell me what was so funny," he reminded her when she started wiping the counter down.

She glanced up at him and tried to remember what she was thinking about. "Oh, it's just funny that after so many years, I can gauge when it's time to start closing down without glancing at a clock."

She watched Cole tilt his head a little and nod. "I guess it's a lot like the way I can tell that a good wave is coming." He smiled at her as she chuckled.

"I guess." She allowed herself to lean against the bar for a moment. "It must be nice to have a job where you are out in the sun all day." She sighed.

He shrugged his shoulders. "Surfing really isn't a job.

Modeling. Now that's a job." He shook his head. "Everyone thinks it's an easy job." He shook his head.

She laughed. "It must be rough, standing around in your underwear all day."

He sighed and shook his head, then turned and said goodbye to Shelly and Marcus, who were leaving.

"You didn't answer my question about Roman," Marcus said to Cole.

"I didn't?" Cole frowned and then grew quiet.

"No," Marcus finally said. "We got interrupted by the fight."

"Oh, right." He chuckled. "That was a crazy one. Did you see how that guy…"

"Cole," Marcus demanded.

"Right." Cole shook his head and sighed. "He's still in Atlanta, I guess."

"You guess?" Marcus leaned on the bar and glared at his brother.

"Yeah, I mean. I haven't actually *spoken* to him."

"Well, what can you tell me." Marcus crossed his arms over his chest and waited.

"He's not home." Cole smiled and leaned back.

"I know that. When will he be home?"

"Why?" Cole asked. Wendy stifled a giggle. She knew when Cole was avoiding answering. She didn't know why he was, but he was doing a terrible job at it tonight.

Marcus rolled his eyes. "Fine, if you're not going to tell me, I'll have Aunt…"

"No!" Cole jumped off the stool and took his brother's shoulders. "Don't you dare."

Marcus shrugged his shoulders. "Fine, then spill."

Cole glanced around and sighed. "Fine, but I'm

waiting until Cassey's done." He nodded to where their sister was busy setting chairs on top of the tables.

"Okay." Marcus glanced at Shelly, who nodded.

"We can wait. I'm not that tired." She smiled.

By the time Wendy finished cleaning and closing out, Cassey was finished as well. They all stood around the bar and waited to hear Cole's big secret.

"He's gone to find Marissa." He left out the part about him finding her. He knew he was betraying Marcus and Cassey, but he'd made Roman a promise. Besides, he wasn't too sure if he believed Roman himself. After all, his brother had, in the last eight years, claimed to have seen her over three dozen times. Of course, no one else had, and half of those times, it had ended up being some woman who only looked like their long-lost sister.

"Is that all?" Cassey sighed. Cole could see the sadness flood into his sister's eye and hoped more than anything that Roman had indeed found Marissa.

"Why didn't he tell us?" Marcus sighed. "I mean; he's taken several of these trips." He used air quotes and looked like a complete dork doing it.

Cole laughed and shook his head. "Guess he didn't want to have to see you do that." He mimicked his brother.

Marcus laughed. "Bite me." Everyone laughed harder.

"Look, maybe he wanted some time. I mean, he's been working his ass off the last few months." Everyone nodded in agreement. "Just taking care of Spring Haven is a full-time job. And he's been helping out with Paradise

Construction and now with your new place." He nodded to Marcus and Shelly.

They both looked at one another. "He's been such a help." Shelly sighed. "He deserves a break."

"Maybe he's just taking a few weeks off." He shrugged his shoulders and started believing the lie himself.

"Okay," Marcus nodded. "We'll keep this to ourselves. But we have to stand unified on the Fourth."

"Oh!" Cassey groaned. "What are we going to say to Dad and Julie?" She leaned her head back a little to look up at them.

He shook his head. "He's in Atlanta straightening out some stuff for Spring Haven. That's what he told me to say, so I'm sticking with it." They all nodded.

"Agreed." Marcus nodded, then grabbed Shelly's hand and pulled her towards the door. "Night," he called out over his shoulder.

Just then, two large Styrofoam containers were delivered to the bar.

"Ready?" Wendy wrapped them up in a bag and nodded to him.

"Sure, is one of those for me?" He reached for them, only to have his hand slapped away playfully.

"If you're good." She laughed. "Night." She waved to Cassey, who watched them leave with a frown on her lips.

"Later. We will talk about this later," she warned as he followed Wendy out of the door. Now he had a whole other conversation in his future to dread.

CHAPTER 8

They walked slowly along the dark boardwalk, hand in hand. He'd won the small battle about carrying the bag of food a few feet outside of the bar. She loved the coolness of the breeze that was rushing off the water that night and enjoyed the feel of his hand in hers.

"Do you always walk to work?" he asked as they hit the street.

"Sure, saves on gas." She chuckled. "Why?"

She watched him shrug his shoulders. "It's just the thought of you walking home in the dark…"

She laughed. "This is Surf Breeze, not Miami."

"Still, there are psychos everywhere."

"True." She nodded. "I can take care of myself."

Sarcastic laughter burst from him. "Did you learn self-defense in yoga?"

She glanced at him sideways. "No, but I learned to shoot at gun school." She tapped her small purse and smiled.

"Carrying?" He nodded. "Yeah, you would." He shook his head.

"What does that mean?" She stopped and looked at him, crossing her arms over her chest.

"Nothing. It's just smart."

She looked at his face to make sure he wasn't being sarcastic and then nodded when she saw the sincerity in his eyes.

"What made you start?" He reached for her hand and continued to walk.

She shrugged her shoulders. "It was Alan's idea." He glanced at her and she could tell he was waiting for the story. She sighed. "Okay, it was after I'd been sort of stalked." She felt his hand tighten in hers. "But," she jumped in quickly, "that was back at the Flora-Bama bar. That place was crazy during spring break."

He stopped her just outside her door. "And now you walk to your condo every night at"—he glanced down and frowned— "one-thirty in the morning with nothing but what I can only presume is the smallest gun possible." He glanced down at her small purse.

She chuckled. "Yes, and I live in a town the size of a shoe box."

He shook his head. "This place gets pretty crazy. Did you see how many people were in there tonight? It was almost packed out on a Monday."

She nodded and smiled at him as she wrapped her arms around his shoulders. "Do you want to fight about it?"

She knew the smile cost him, but it was worth it to see his lips turn up. "Later," he mumbled before his lips touched hers. "Now, I'm too hungry to argue."

She nodded. "Ditto."

When she opened her door, she enjoyed the fact that she'd kept her small place clean. She no longer had to rush around cleaning before a man came over. She'd spent most of her morning organizing the rest of her place using everything she'd bought the day before. She even had a small list of items that would further organize the place.

"You've cleaned up the place," he said, walking in and looking around. "Is this new?" He walked over to her table and picked up a small ball covered in dried leaves. She'd picked up the bowl and balls to decorate her table along with the new placemats.

"Yeah, I bought them yesterday."

"Cool." He tossed it back in the bowl. "I guess you like this kind of stuff." He looked around again and she could tell he was noticing the other new things she'd put out. She turned and started unloading their dinner, putting the sandwiches out on plates.

"Here." She reached in and shoved a cheese stick in her mouth. "You can start with these." She handed him the chips and salsa. "I don't know what Sam puts in the salsa, but it's addictive." She scooped some up with her cheese stick and moaned.

"Lime," he said, scooping some up with a chip.

"What?" She frowned at him.

He shrugged his shoulders. "I asked."

"So, did I." She crossed her arms over her chest.

He chuckled. "I asked after signing his kid's surfboard for him."

She growled. "Famous people suck." She turned back towards her task. "I bet you can get anything you want. All you'd have to do is walk in wearing a pair of shorts and no shirt and they'd give you the key to the city."

He chuckled. "It does have its advantages." She felt him take her hips with his hands. She sighed as her knees went weak and she leaned back against his chest.

"This is not because of that." She enjoyed herself for just a moment.

"If I thought it was, I wouldn't be here," he said against her hair.

"What about all the others?" She turned in his arms, looking up at him.

"What others?" He took her mouth with his as his hands reached around and pulled her closer. She felt his arousal against her hip and instantly felt herself go warm. The food sat on the counter, forgotten, as they hungrily enjoyed each other.

"Cole," she begged, trying to pull him closer. "Don't make me wait again."

"No," he said as he started to tug her shirt over her head. "Not this time."

He walked her towards the back of her condo, and when her knees hit the edge of her bed, he stopped her from falling back. She reached for him, pulling his shirt over his head as he watched her. She shook her head. "This should be illegal." She ran her hand over his chest as he chuckled.

"I agree." His finger lightly played over her chest, causing her eyes to close. His finger hooked under her bra, sending it off her shoulder. She sighed at the release of the weight and then moaned when his finger followed the curve. She felt herself sway a little, and then he was taking her hips and guiding her down to the bed.

He lay beside her, running his hands lightly over her skin. The tight shorts she'd worn to work were peeled slowly off her until she lay there in nothing, but a matching bra and panty set she'd splurged on the day before. When she looked up, she frowned. He was still wearing his shorts. She started to tug them off, only to have his hands take hers and move them above her head, holding her still.

He chuckled when she frowned at him. "Trust me, we'll get to that. For now, I want to enjoy you." He moved until both of her hands were encased in one of his. "Who would have thought." His eyes traveled over her.

"What?" It came out as a whisper. How could she have known that just having him look at her would turn her on so much?

"That I'd stray from being an ass man." He shook his head as his eyes and freehand traveled over her powder-pink bra. She arched her back, trying to get him to move faster. "Easy." He chuckled as he slowly moved the strap off her other shoulder. Using just one finger, he swirled her shoulder, traveled across her collarbone, down until he lightly moved the lace down, exposing her. She felt her nipples pucker in the cool air or maybe it was because his eyes were hungrily eating her up.

Her hands were still caught up in his above her head, but she knew she could break free if she tried. When his fingers traveled down behind her, she arched so he could unclasp her bra.

"Okay, definitely rethinking this whole ass man thing." He chuckled as he tossed her bra aside. She giggled and arched a little more for him.

"Touch me," she begged, needing to feel his skin on hers. So far, since he'd freed her, all he'd done was look.

His free hand lightly scraped down her shoulder until

he brushed against her chest. Dual moans sounded, and she thought for sure she'd burst if he didn't touch her more. Then his warm mouth was on her, sucking and licking her, and she broke her hands-free to bury them deep in his hair.

"Yes," she moaned. Needing the warmth of him next to her, she wrapped her legs around his hips and moved against him. She could feel his desire for her and had to have more. But when she tried again to remove his shorts, he stopped her with a chuckle.

"Not yet. I'm enjoying my new-found obsessions." He chuckled against her nipple. His hands reached up and took her wrists, pulling them aside.

"Cole," she warned, not wanting to have to wrestle him down. He just chuckled again, then gasped when she flipped him over and straddled him quickly. "You asked for it." She smiled down at him as she pinned his hips to the bed.

Cole was trying to go slow. After all, how could you tell a woman that if she touched him, the evening would end too soon? He held back a chuckle. This had never happened to him before. He'd always been suave in bed before her. Now, however, if she did manage to pull his shorts off, he knew that would be that.

He looked up at her and groaned. Her breasts had seemed perfect when she was lying there in front of him but hovering above him they were even better. He closed his eyes and felt himself get even harder than before, which was something he hadn't ever experienced.

"Wendy," he croaked out between clenched teeth, "if you don't let me lead, this isn't going to last long."

She chuckled. "Lie there and take my punishment." She ran her hands up his sides, setting off his tickle spots, but he bit his tongue and held back the chuckles. "You think it's okay to torture a woman like this, well, let me give you a taste of your own medicine." She pulled his arms above his head and then held them both with one of hers. "Don't move," she warned.

His eyes were closed, so he just nodded.

"Look at me," she said against his skin. "Watch what I do to you." Her mouth was on his chest, along with her free hand. His eyes zeroed in on her mouth as she ran her tongue over his flat nipple. He felt her hips pinning his down and couldn't stop the desire from flooding into each and every vein in his body.

"Mmm, I love these." She ran her fingertips over his pecs, then down his arms, and continued past his stomach. "And here…" Her mouth replaced her hands as she ran her lips over his hip then lightly tugged on his shorts. When he moved to stop her, she pushed his hands away gently. "Remember, it's my turn."

He leaned his head back and closed his eyes and tried to think of a million things other than what she was doing to him, so he would last longer. When her mouth hovered above his cock, he felt his entire body shiver with desire. Then her lips touched him, and he was sure he'd never experienced as much want as he did right then. His hands went into her hair, holding her, guiding her as she took her time pleasing him. When he didn't think he could stand it any longer, he hooked his hands under her arms and pulled her up his body as she smiled down at him.

"Enough," he growled as he flipped their positions. When he had her back underneath him, he felt a little more centered. Then she wrapped her legs around his hips and he felt himself pressed up against her core. His sight actually went a little gray around the edges.

Reaching over, he pulled his wallet from his shorts and had the rubber on himself quickly. He came back over her, and she wrapped her arms around his shoulders. He kissed her until he felt her own shiver of desire. When he slid slowly into her, he couldn't stop the moan from escaping his lips or the growl that came after as he heard her own moan of delight.

"Hold onto me," he said as he started to move. He watched her blue eyes open slightly and then focus on his face. He hadn't known what it would do to him, seeing her eyes go soft as he moved inside her. When they slid closed a few moments later, he watched her throw her head back and lose herself and quickly followed.

CHAPTER 9

*L*aying there looking up at her ceiling, with Cole breathing lightly in her hair, she started wondering just what the heck she'd done. Her mind kept playing over how she'd gone from hating him, to bringing him home and… she closed her eyes and held back a groan.

When he moved, she thought he would roll off the bed to leave, but instead, he snuggled next to her, pulling her closer to his chest. She had to admit, it felt pretty damn great. Her arms went around him as her face was buried in the hard muscles of his chest. He smelled like the ocean, which only reminded her of who he was.

Sighing, she closed her eyes for just a moment and heard her stomach growl. Then he chuckled.

"I guess I pulled us away from the food. Hang on." He rolled away from the bed and she instantly missed his warmth, the feel of him, and even the subtle scent of the surf.

She reached down and pulled up the covers until her

shoulders were covered as she heard him banging around in her kitchen. When he walked back into the room completely naked with a large plate balanced on each hand, her mouth went dry. How could any woman ever say no to a man like Cole?

"What?" He stopped halfway across the room and looked down at her.

She shook her head and chuckled. "I've never had food served to me in bed by an underwear model in the buff before.

He chuckled and walked over to sit next to her on the bed. "Well, then we both are doing something new since I've never served food to anyone in bed before."

She reached up and took a plate from him. He moved over and sat next to her under the blankets.

"Too bad you don't have a TV in here." He frowned, checking out her blank wall across from her bed.

"The bedroom is for sleeping," she said between bites.

He chuckled. "And other fun things." He wiggled his eyebrows at her, causing her to laugh.

"Besides, I spent almost an entire month's worth of tips on the one out there." She nodded to the living room where her big flat-screen TV hung on the wall.

He frowned for a moment and then shrugged his shoulders. "I guess it's better than the one I have."

She chuckled. "You don't own—"

"I know." He interrupted and smiled at her.

She thought for just a moment that she saw something sad cross his eyes, but then he was cracking a joke about something else and the moment was gone.

"So, are you going to tell me what's really up?" She

leaned back against her padded headboard and glanced at him.

"With what?" He frowned a little.

She smiled. "So, you're keeping two secrets then." She nodded when she saw the truth in his eyes. "Spill." She crossed her arms over her chest.

"I have no idea what you're talking about." He took her plate and set it, along with his own, on her nightstand. Then he leaned in and started raining kisses along her shoulder blade.

She chuckled. "Trying to get out of telling me what you forgot to mention to your family tonight?"

He shrugged his shoulders and looked up at her. "Is it working?" he asked as he pulled the sheet away and placed his mouth on her. She felt her eyes roll to the back as her body started responding to him.

When she moaned and grabbed his hair with her hands, he chuckled. "I'll take that as a yes."

This time, however, she wasn't willing to wait and pulled him down and fused her lips to his. Her hands rushed over his body, feeling every strong line, every strained cord as he tried to control himself.

When she pushed his shoulders, he fell back and let her slide over him. This time, she reached in her nightstand and enjoyed watching his face as she slid a condom slowly on him. When she moved over him, his hands went to her hips. His nails dug into her as she started to move her hips slowly. She threw her head back and let the rhythm build until he pulled her down to him and his mouth covered her cries of pleasure.

"That's it," he moaned against her lips. "Come for me."

She couldn't have denied him, not when he was holding her and kissing her to oblivion. After she convulsed around him, he moved until she lay underneath him and then continued to use his mouth on her until she felt herself building again.

When his hand moved down between them, she fell over the edge and marveled at the sound of him calling her name.

When Cole woke up, his senses and thoughts were instantly flooded with Wendy. His face was next to her hair and with every breath he took, he could smell her sexy scent. Her naked, warm back was pressed up against his front, making his body ache.

He pulled her closer and could tell the moment she started to wake up. He felt her shoulders tense, and she sighed and relaxed back into him.

"Having regrets?" he asked as he ran his hands over her skin.

She shook her head no. "You?"

He chuckled. "Does this feel like I'm having second thoughts?" He pushed himself closer to her and heard her moan.

When he moved her leg higher, exposing her to him as he ran a finger over her sweet spot, she cried out and started slowly grinding her hips. He loved the way she responded to his touch; he was completely addicted to her. Her taste, her smell, the feel of her body wrapped around his. When he slowly pushed inside her, her hands fisted in the sheets as she gasped.

He couldn't have known that making love to Wendy would have touched him so much. To see and hear her responses to him... it was beyond anything he'd ever imagined.

When he felt her release, he joined her and then lay there holding her until he felt her drift off again. His mind refused to shut down, especially since he could see the sun trying to break through her thick curtains.

He knew she probably wasn't a morning person—how could she be, working the hours she did? —but Cole lived for the early mornings. His body called for him to move, but his mind and heart wanted to stay in bed with Wendy all day.

A few minutes later, it was his stomach that finally pulled him away from her sleeping body. He showered quickly and then walked into her kitchen with one thing on his mind. All of the Grayton men knew how to cook; their mother and Julie had seen to that.

Moving around in her kitchen quietly, he made scrambled eggs, French toast, and bacon. It must have been the bacon smell that finally caused Wendy to walk out of the bedroom wearing a tight little shirt and shorts, making his mouth water.

"Morning." He smiled over at her while trying to keep his eyes from zeroing in on her breasts. Man, why had he believed he'd been an ass man before?

"Morning." She groaned and glanced up at the clock on her wall and groaned again. "It *is* still morning."

He chuckled. "I know. Sorry." He scooped a spoonful of eggs onto a plate for her. "You can go back to bed."

She shrugged her shoulders. "Not knowing there's

bacon in here." She sat down at the table and tucked her legs underneath her.

He smiled and set a plate in front of her. "There's more than just bacon." He leaned down and kissed her until he felt her melt under his lips. "Mmm, now that I've had dessert." He smiled, then made himself a plate and sat next to her.

"This is really good," she said after a bite.

"Thanks." He scooped up some eggs and enjoyed the spicy flavor. He loved adding salsa to almost everything.

"I have never had salsa on eggs before." She glanced at him.

He chuckled. "My brothers got me started on it years ago."

"Oh?" She glanced at him in question.

He smiled. "Marcus decided they were going to play a trick on me. One morning they piled a heap of salsa on everything on my plate." He shrugged his shoulders. "They had no clue that I'd love it."

She smiled. "Backfired, didn't it?"

He nodded. "So, now they even have it on their eggs and fries."

Her eyebrows shot up. "I'll have to try that too."

He smiled. "Better than ketchup."

She shook her head. "I don't know. I'm a ketchup-aholic." He chuckled. "So, what are your plans for the day?"

He thought about it. "First thing I'm going to do is turn off my cell phone." Her eyebrows shot up in question. "So, Marcus can't recruit me again today." She smiled. "Second thing, I'm going to grab my paddle board and head out." He looked over at her. "Want to join me?"

He watched her head tilt and her eyes move back towards the clock. Then she sighed and looked around. "Sure, why not. I'm not working until six tonight."

He smiled. "Perfect. I'll clean up while you get ready." He reached over and took her empty plate.

"You're going to do dishes?" She shook her head as she got up. "I just can't get used to a man who does dishes," she said as she walked out of the room.

He smiled and watched her leave. Maybe he hadn't completely changed from an ass man yet, he thought as he watched her walk away from him in the tight shorts.

By the time, they hit the water it was almost eleven. The sun was high, and the heat level was higher. He carried the longboard through the hot, white sand as Wendy followed him with the paddles.

"It's a green day." She nodded to the beach flag. "I love green days." She sighed and jogged a little to catch up with him.

He looked over and frowned. "Yeah, I guess."

She chuckled. "I bet you love seeing the red flag fly." She shook her head.

He smiled. "Red means waves."

"It also means dangerous currents." She shook her head. "You know, the kind that can drag you under or out to sea."

He shrugged. "Green is boring."

She chuckled as he set the paddle board down next to the calm water. "Not everything boring is bad."

He shrugged his shoulders and took the paddles from

her. "I suppose." He set the paddles down and then pulled her next to him. She looked sexy as hell in a green bikini with cut-off shorts. She'd pulled her hair back and it hung over her shoulder in a sexy twist. "But I live for danger." He leaned down and kissed her lips, feeling the familiar zing jump through his body. He usually got the same feeling riding down a big wave during a storm. Smiling, he pulled back and picked up the paddles. "Well, come on." He handed her one. "Let's get out on the calm, boring water."

She chuckled and nodded then followed him out into the warm water.

By the time they pulled back onto the beach, he had to admit that it hadn't been boring out on the water with Wendy. They had laughed, joked, and talked more than he ever had with a woman.

Of course, they'd ended up in the water when he'd tried to push her playfully in. He'd been surprised that she'd easily sidestepped his move, and they'd both gone flying off the board into the water.

"You have some moves," he admitted when they finally pulled the board back onto the sand.

She smiled. "Thanks, you're not so bad either."

He chuckled. "You should see me on a smaller board." He glanced at the calm water and nodded. "And on bigger waves."

"I have." She frowned and glanced away from him.

"And?" He tugged her into the sand and sat down next to her.

She shrugged her shoulders and put her knees up to her chest. "You're a great surfer."

"But?" he prodded as he used his finger to turn her face towards his.

She shrugged her shoulders again and then sighed. "Why do you surf the storms? I mean…" She shook her head. "The one in Australia last year." She leaned back on her hands and watched a group of teenagers playing in the water.

"Australia was a blast." He smiled.

"Yeah." He heard the disappointment in her voice.

"Hey." He pulled on her until she was almost in his lap. "I wasn't in any danger."

"Right," she said dryly, holding her hands between them on his chest.

"It was a small storm." He smiled. "Besides, that shot Carl took of me made the cover of three magazines."

She nodded. "Yeah, but I saw what it did to Cassey."

He tilted his head in question. "She worried the entire time you were gone. Not to mention Roman and Marcus." She sighed and ran a finger down his arm. "I can tell that they can't wait until you retire."

"Retire?" He laughed. "Me? Retire? Yeah, right. I'm never going to retire."

He thought he heard her sigh, but he was too busy kissing that sweet mouth of hers to be sure.

CHAPTER 10

Working at a bar had its ups and downs. The ups… it was great money. The downs… you had to work and put on a smile no matter how bad you felt. Wendy's heart just wasn't into working that night. Especially since Cole had mentioned that he had some things to do that night and wouldn't be in. Not that she was expecting him to come in and sit in his sister's place every night.

But after the statement he'd made earlier, she was seriously beginning to doubt why she was with him. After all, she knew exactly what she was getting into with him.

Had she really expected him to change that much? He'd been living on the edge for so long before she'd met him, there was little she could do to change that part of who he was. Nor would she really want to. After all, he was really a great surfer.

She'd watched videos of him often enough to know that he was one of the best in the water. He'd won more trophies than any other surfer in the last ten years. He even had a surf move named after him.

She sighed and finished an order for a large family that had come in an hour before sunset. There wasn't a band playing tonight and the place seemed so dull.

She supposed she understood what Cole meant when he said boring isn't fun. After all, she lived for the nights when it was standing room only around the bar—loud music pumping, people yelling their orders. She even kind of like watching a fight break out. Not that she was into violence, just drama.

Sighing, she leaned against the bar and thought about how boring the rest of the night was going to be. There were less than a dozen tables occupied and glancing out the windows and seeing the perfect sunset, she doubted there would be a huge crowd coming in anytime soon.

She watched Cassey walk down the stairs and frowned when she noticed the worried look on her boss's face.

"Hey," she said, handing over a cold can of Coke, Cassey's favorite drink.

"Hi." She picked up the can and took a large sip. "Slow night, huh?"

She nodded. "It should pick up this weekend. You know, for the Fourth."

She nodded. "Yeah, we're expecting record crowds. Luke's hotel is completely booked."

"Wow." She whistled.

"I've got the schedule pinned up." She nodded towards the back hallway where a bulletin board sat with the schedule. "Sorry, I've got you working a double."

She chuckled. "I did ask for it, remember?"

"Yeah, but that was before…" Cassey dropped off and took another sip of her drink.

"Before I started seeing your brother?"

Cassey nodded and looked away.

"You don't have to warn me again about him." She leaned on the counter. "I know what I'm getting into."

"I know." Cassey sighed and sat on a stool, then rested her elbows up on the bar and put her chin in her hands. "It's just that… Well, Cole isn't like Marcus or Roman."

She chuckled and nodded. "Yeah, he's nuts."

Cassey rolled her eyes. "Not what I meant."

"Don't worry, I'm very guarded."

Cassey reached over and touched her hand. "I'm sorry. I won't pry. I love Cole. Very much. But we've all learned to put up with… that side of him."

She smiled. "The side that wants to do everything he can to kill himself?"

Cassey nodded. "Yeah, I guess you're right. He's nuts." They both laughed.

By closing time, her feet and back hurt so much that she rushed home and jumped in a hot bath. The entire night her mind had played over and over the conversation with Cole and the one she'd had with Cassey. By morning, she had barely gotten enough sleep and was pulling herself out of bed for the early shift she had. Okay, so early to her was starting work at one in the afternoon. Still, it was hours earlier than she normally went in since Alan had taken the next two days off. There were other bartenders, but she'd been trying to save up and needed the extra cash.

When she walked in, her eyes hidden from the bright sun in the darkest sunglasses she owned, she was shocked to see her sister sitting at the bar with a drink in her hands.

"Willow?" Her sister turned around and set the almost empty drink down. Rushing over, she took Willow's shoulders and almost fell over when she collapsed against her in tears. Wendy looked at the new bartender, Steven, behind the counter and frowned at him, making a mental note to show him the difference between a fake ID and a real ID.

"What's wrong?" she asked, pulling her sister towards the back break room.

"It's… It's Jake. He…" Willow swallowed and closed her eyes.

"Who is Jake?" She asked, pushing her sister into a chair.

"My boyfriend." She glared up at her.

"Oh." Wendy felt relieved to know the guy's name again. "What about him?"

"He's gone into the army."

Wendy sat down next to her sister and waited. "And?"

"And nothing!" Willow shot her another look.

"Well, isn't that a good thing. I mean…"

"No, it's not a good thing!" Willow stood up and crossed her arms over her chest as she walked the small room. "He's leaving for basic next week."

"Honey, I think boot camp will be good for Jake." She pulled on her sister's arms until she sat down again. "Besides, you're too young to…"

"What?" Willow glared at her. "Jake and I are in love. Just because you don't know what it's like doesn't mean other people can't enjoy it."

"Willow," she warned.

"I don't care." She tossed off her hands and stood up again. "We're meant to be together."

"Then why did he join the army without asking you

first?" she burst out. The second the words left her lips, she regretted them.

Willow turned and glared at her. "He had to." She bawled. "It was that or…"

"Prison?" Wendy leaned back in her chair and crossed her arms over her chest.

"No! His parents were going to cut him off. Financially." She frowned down at her fingers.

Wendy laughed. "Really? He chose going into the army over getting a job and working?"

Willow just glared at her some more as Wendy shook her head and walked over to stand in front of her sister.

Willow was about two inches taller than Wendy. They both had the long blonde hair, dark blue eyes, and skin that belonged on models. But where Wendy had been forced to be more levelheaded, Willow still acted like a spoiled child. Wendy blamed herself for that. Everything Willow wanted as a child, Wendy had bent over backward to get her. That was until she reached her teens.

Then something had shifted in the relationship. Wendy had started treating Willow like a sister instead of her responsibility, and Willow had started to turn away. It had been shortly after their father's death, so Wendy didn't know what the real cause was, only that they had grown apart.

"I'm sorry about Jake. But a little time apart won't damage a relationship that is meant to be."

Willow looked at her and sighed. "You're right."

"Now, since you're down here…" She glanced over at the schedule and frowned as she calculated. "How about a quick lunch with your sister?"

Willow glanced at her phone, then back up. "I can't. I'm supposed to be at work in two hours."

"Then why did you come here? Instead of my place?"

Willow sighed and shrugged her shoulders. "I thought you'd be working."

"You could have called." She put her hands on her hips.

"I didn't want to bother you." Willow turned and started to pick up her purse.

"Willow." She waited until her sister turned and looked back at her. "Someday we're going to have to talk about this."

Willow's eyebrows shot up, and she slowly nodded when she understood. "Not today. I have enough going on right now."

Wendy nodded and sighed. "Soon, okay? I miss my sister."

Willow turned and walked out of the break room without another word. Wendy sat back down. She felt like crying. Why would her sister come to her for advice on her love life but not open up to her about their relationship?

She sat in the break room until she felt like she had everything back under control, then went out to start her shift and yell at Steven for giving her nineteen-year-old sister a beer.

Over the next few days, Cole was completely busy. Not only did he have family obligations, but he had work as well. He had a new contract with a big swim clothing company that had a new line of shorts they wanted him to model. He spent two whole days in a photography studio outside of Panama City that he always used, feeling like he was on display.

Every chance he had, he would text or call Wendy. He could tell by the tone of her messages that something was up, but every time he asked, she would sidestep the conversation.

Finally, early Friday, he drove over to her place and knocked on the door. When she didn't answer, he walked down to the bar and grill.

Seeing her behind the counter in a tight black tank top with at least a dozen guys hovering around her did something to him. She was smiling and laughing as she flipped a bottle over her head and caught it upside down as the liquor poured into the glasses on the bar top. All of the men cheered and clapped, sending more deadly waves of jealousy shooting through every vein in his body.

When he walked up to the bar, he thought he had himself back under control, until one of the men reached across and took her hand in his. He pushed his way through the group of men and bumped the guy aside with his hip.

"Oops, sorry," he mumbled as Wendy's eyes moved to his. He saw her frown a little as she was pouring more drinks.

"Hey!" the guy, who was apparently very drunk, said loudly before turning to look at him. Cole could tell the second the guy recognized him and groaned inwardly knowing what was coming next.

"You're Cole Grayton." He almost yelled it over the music.

"Yeah." He nodded and turned to Wendy to try and

head the guy off by ordering a drink. But he wouldn't be that lucky.

"Hey, look," he called out to his buddies. "This here"—he threw his arm over Cole's shoulder and turned him away from the bar towards his friends— "is Cole freaking Grayton. Best damn surfer in the states."

"So, did you get us our beers yet?" one of his friends called from the back of the group.

"Shut up, Jeff," the drunk guy called back. "Hey, man, I've watched every one of your competitions. I'm a surfer myself."

"That's good." He tried to remove the guy's arm from his shoulders, only to have the man grab him again. "I'm buying you a drink." He shook him and turned back to the bar. "What are you having?"

Cole sighed and shook his head at Wendy. It was hard to stay mad at a guy that was this drunk, especially when he was a fan.

The next hour was a blur of drinks. Every chance he got, he would look Wendy's way. She seemed very busy and looked like she was loving it.

Finally, after the large crowd of people left, he could talk to her. There were still plenty of orders for her to fill, but in between, she would stop off and lean on the counter.

"So, how did the shoot go?"

He shrugged his shoulders. "Okay. I have a box of new shorts to wear." He smiled.

She laughed. "Good, maybe now you'll throw away those ugly green ones."

He shook his head. "Those have taken me through everything. I wouldn't have won my first Junior ISA award without them."

She shook her head and sighed. "Seriously?"

"Speaking of which, I've got this thing next week and was wondering if you wanted to go with me." He leaned closer to her and reached out to take her hand in his.

"What thing and where?" She glanced down at their hands and smiled.

"It's the Ku Ikaika Challenge in Hawaii."

He watched her chin drop a little. "Hawaii?" She blinked a few times.

"Yeah, why not?" He ran his thumb over the inside of her wrist and felt her heart skip a beat.

"I… I've never been anywhere."

He chuckled. "Honey, you are somewhere. We all are."

She shook her head. "I've never really been outside of… well, here." She glanced around.

"Isn't it about time then?" He tugged on her hand until her eyes focused on him. "I'll talk to my sister and see if she can clear your schedule." He started to get up, only to have her tug him back.

"Hold on." She frowned at him. "I can deal with my own schedule and I haven't said yes yet."

He chuckled and nodded. "Okay, fine. Say yes."

He watched her bite her bottom lip and glance around the almost empty bar. "Okay," she smiled, and he could see the excitement rush into her eyes.

He nodded. "Great, we leave on Tuesday."

She frowned. "But that's the day after the Fourth."

He nodded. "Yeah?"

She sighed and closed her eyes. "I'm pulling a double the day before."

"You work on the Fourth?" He frowned and sat back down as she nodded.

"But I thought you were going to go hang with my family. Julie invited you."

She nodded. "I forgot that I'd requested it earlier. Besides, I could use the money to pay off the shopping spree I went on last weekend."

He sighed. "Is it too late to change it?"

She nodded.

"Okay." He glanced around. "But get the following four days off. We're hitting the islands."

She nodded and smiled.

CHAPTER 11

ourth of July came, and Wendy was pumped. She had her bags packed already as she headed out for the early shift. When she arrived, she was shocked to see Cole leaning against the railing of the boardwalk. He had a bag and a holder with three coffee cups in his hands.

"Morning." He smiled.

She glanced down at her watch and smiled. "Yes, it is."

"Here, this one is for you." He handed her the cup of coffee. "Caramel Macchiato."

She smiled and took a sip. The richness sank into her. "Who's that for?"

Cole looked down at the remaining cup. "Double-chocolate-chip Frappuccino for Cass. And these"—he wiggled the bag he held— "are donuts. I didn't know what kind you like, so I grabbed a few different kinds."

She smiled. "Anything with chocolate on it."

He nodded and then started walking towards the main

doors as she followed. "What are you doing here? Besides being a delivery boy?" She held open the door for him.

"Helping out."

"What?" She jogged to catch up to him as she took another sip of the rich drink.

"When Cassey told me that she was short staffed, I figured I'd help out." He smiled. "Meet your new busboy for the day."

She laughed. "The last time you bused, you ended up breaking half the dishes."

He frowned and nodded. "That's because Marcus was working alongside me that day. He kept tripping me."

She chuckled and shook her head. "I just bet."

His eyebrows shot up. "Do you?" He set the coffee and donuts down and pulled her closer to him. "What will you give me if I don't break a dish all day?" He leaned down and kissed her once.

She smiled, liking the game. "How about, if you don't break a dish, any dish, all day long, I'll let you see what I bought last weekend at Victoria's Secret."

She felt him stiffen a little and couldn't stop her smile from growing.

"And if I lose?"

She thought about it. "You have to model for me in those new 'shorts' you have."

He smiled and nodded. "Deal."

When she heard the first glass drop, she smiled. By the third, she was laughing so hard, she almost dropped a glass herself. With each new shattered piece of dishware, she could just imagine his silent curses.

Around four o'clock that afternoon, Cole's whole family, minus Roman, walked in the door. Cassey had reserved the back booth a few minutes earlier, so the family walked over and sat down in their usual spot. Cole walked over to them and then came to her.

"Do you have a break?" He leaned over and touched her hand.

"Sure." She smiled. After making sure Alan and Steven had the bar area covered, she walked over to the table and sat with his family.

"It's a shame Roman had to work." Julie frowned a little and looked towards Cole.

"He should be home soon enough," Marcus put in, then quickly changed the subject to how his and Shelly's house was almost done, and how their wedding plans were moving along as well. That kept everyone busy talking for the next forty minutes until their dinner arrived.

After the food arrived, the conversation moved on to their trip to Hawaii the next day. Then it was time for her to get back to work. As she stood up, Cole stood up too.

"Well, back to work." He tugged on her arm, just as his dad started asking about Roman again. "Whew, that was close," he whispered to her as he walked towards the bar.

She chuckled, then glanced over her shoulder and saw Marcus glaring at the back of Cole's head. "Your brother is shooting daggers at your back."

He chuckled. "He'll get over it. Besides, he owes me after all the hard work I did on his place."

She smiled when he pulled her into his arms. "Only a few more hours to go until we are free for five days."

"Five?" She frowned. "I thought you said four?"

"Uh, yeah, about that."

"I only took four days off."

He chuckled. "Why do you think I'm working today? I

had to promise Cassey I'd help out, so you could have an extra day off, with pay."

"With pay?" She glanced over at the booth and was shocked to see the entire table watching them, smiling. Cassey winked at her and then turned back to her husband.

"I have the best boss in the world." She sighed.

After that, the music turned loud, and the crowd flowed in until just before closing time. There was a slight lull when the fireworks were being set off, but shortly after, everyone flocked back in.

When Cassie finally locked the front doors, Wendy sat down in a chair with a cold beer and propped her feet up.

"You made it through the day." She smiled over at Cole, who was doing the same thing, except he had a Bushwhacker instead of a beer.

"Was there ever any doubt?" Then he frowned. "I can explain the dishes."

She chuckled and shook her head. "Don't be a sore loser."

He smiled. "Who says I am? Just—" Her laughing interrupted him. "Fine." He crossed his arms over his chest, but he was smiling.

"Cole never could stand to lose." Cassey joined them at the table. "Remember the time I bet you at basketball?"

A burst of laughter escaped from Wendy. She looked over at Cole and smiled. "Sorry."

He frowned at her. "It wasn't like that. I had a broken arm."

Cassey laughed. "The summer before. He kept complaining that it was still hurting him, but before I showed up, he'd whooped both Roman's and Marcus's butts."

Wendy couldn't help it, she smiled. "Sore loser."

He frowned and set his empty glass down. "Come on, we'd better get some sleep if we expect to catch our plane tomorrow morning." He tugged on her hands, pulling her up as she smiled over at Cassey.

"Have a great trip."

She nodded and then tugged on his arm until he stopped. "Thanks for the extra day."

Cassey stood and hugged her. "Don't worry about it. I'm glad you're finally taking a real vacation." Wendy smiled as Cole continued to tug on her arm until they were outside.

"What's the big hurry?" she asked as he walked quickly towards her place.

He glanced over at her and smiled. "I'm tired."

"Right." She chuckled. "You don't look tired. Are you eager to do a little modeling for me?"

He smiled again. "No, maybe I just want to get horizontal." He pulled her close as they walked.

"Oh?" She felt her knees almost give out.

Before she knew it, they were at her front door and he was taking the keys from her to open the locks. Then he pulled her through her door and pushed her up against the other side. Cole's mouth covered hers as she sighed and wrapped her arms around his shoulders.

"I couldn't keep my eyes off you all night," he moaned against her skin. "I kept thinking about getting my hands on you." He ran his hands up and down her sides and then started tugging her shirt over her head. "Oh, god," he said when her bright pink bra was exposed.

"You like?" she whispered, her eyes on his. She smiled when he just nodded, his eyes glued to her chest.

"Is this what you bought?" He ran a finger down the strap.

She nodded. "Not the one I was going to show you… had you not broken almost a dozen dishes tonight."

She smiled as he groaned. "Damn." He leaned close and placed his lips on the curve of her shoulder.

She leaned her head back against the door and enjoyed his mouth traveling over her skin, heating it up. He hiked her skirt up until he could grip her naked hips and he leaned closer. She could feel how hard and excited he was. When she quickly pulled his shorts off his hips, he chuckled and then sighed as she gripped him firmly.

He pushed her farther against the door, spreading her legs as he moved between them. His fingers went between them, gliding below her matching pink panties. He pulled them aside quickly.

When he dipped a finger into her, she cried out and dug her nails into his shoulders.

"Yes, that's it." He breathed next to her ear. "Enjoy."

She nodded, not able to do anything but enjoy the feeling of him next to her, holding her up as he pleasured her.

Finally, when she didn't think she could stand it any longer, she felt him slide into her quickly. She wrapped her leg around his hip and pulled him closer. He pounded into her as his mouth took hers. When she cried out, he was right there with her and groaned her name into her hair.

Then he shocked her by carrying her into the bedroom and slowly removing the rest of her clothes. He threw the covers over them and pulled her closer to his side with his arms wrapped around her.

"Night," he said, kissing her forehead.

She lay there awake for almost an hour. Her mind refused to shut down. She was excited about the trip they were taking in just a few short hours and had so many emotions welling up inside her from hearing Cole lightly snore next to her and feeling his arms wrapped around her tightly.

She'd never experienced such want before. Such need. The few boyfriends she'd had in the past had never treated her like this. Like she was fragile or something to be treasured.

Cole laughed when Wendy's chin dropped as she sat down next to him on the plane.

"First class?" She frowned a little and looked around the cabin.

"Yeah, why not? After all, you did say this was your first flight." He smiled and moved as close to her as the big chairs would allow.

"Yes, but…" She shook her head in disbelief.

"Sit back, relax." He took her hand and she leaned back, her eyes traveling everywhere. "We'll have some wine after we take off."

She shook her head and smiled. "Still can't believe it. I'm going to Hawaii."

He smiled and pulled her hand up to his lips. "We're going."

"Who is this friend we're staying with again?"

"Maka. I stay with him; he stays with me." He shrugged his shoulders. "I've known him since before…" He shrugged his shoulders again.

"Maka? *Maka*?" She gaped at him.

He nodded and smiled. "Yeah, he's going to love that I brought you along."

"Oh?" She started to tug her hand free. "You did tell him?"

He chuckled. "Yes, he knows I'm bringing someone."

"Someone?" She frowned and crossed her arms over her chest. "Really, Cole. How many—?"

Just then the flight attendants started their spiel on safety, and Wendy silently listened. She even pulled out the little pamphlet and followed along. When they were done, she double checked her seat belt and glanced over to make sure his was on. He laughed at her and took her hand again as the plane started to move.

At six o'clock that evening, Hawaiian time, they finally landed on Oahu. After picking up their luggage, they walked out to find Maka standing next to his old Jeep, four surfboards strapped to the roof.

"Aloha, Kaikua`ana." The short, dark-skinned man walked over and hugged Cole. Then his dark eyes zeroed in on Wendy and his white teeth flashed in one of his signature smiles. "So, this is your wahine."

Cole chuckled. "Yes, Wendy is my woman." He pulled her close to his side. "Don't get any ideas," he warned his friend, who just smiled and took Wendy's hand up to his lips.

"Aloha, Ka makani `olu`." He smiled as he placed a kiss on her hand.

"Did you just call her perfect wind?" Cole frowned over at his friend.

"You can pick out your own nickname for her. This one's taken." He took Wendy's arm and walked her towards his Jeep as she chuckled and glanced back at Cole. "Oh, Cole…" Maka glanced back. "Make sure to grab the lady's luggage." He smiled and continued walking as Cole laughed.

"Kakahiaka, my home, is on the other side of O'ahu. Not too far from the North Shore." Maka smiled over at Wendy, who was sitting in the front seat of the Jeep, as Cole held on to the top rails in the back seat. "You will enjoy your time here."

"Thank you for letting us stay." Wendy smiled and glanced back at him.

"It's no problem. Cole and I go way back. Although, I have to say, he's never brought a woman here before." Maka glanced at him in the rear-view mirror.

"Shut up," Cole warned his friend as he held on when they went flying around a corner. "Haven't you learned to drive yet?"

Maka just laughed.

Maka chatted about the island and the landscape for the entire forty-minute trip. The road split the island in half and went right down the middle of the land. They saw homes, small villages, and field after field of farmland, but when they came to the turn where they would start traveling along the shoreline, he watched closely for Wendy's reaction.

She gasped and turned in her seat to face the water. Her blue eyes got bigger as a smile spread on her face.

"Beautiful, isn't it?" He leaned closer, so he could tangle his hands in her hair.

She nodded. "I never imagined." She glanced back at him and he smiled at her and felt a piece of his heart drift to the front seat.

endy stood back as Cole and Maka unloaded the luggage from the Jeep. She couldn't believe her eyes. Maka's house was gorgeous. It was a three-story wall made of glass. Well, at least that's what it looked like from where she was standing.

There were long balconies along the entire front of the house, which faced the beautiful beach and the crystal-clear waters. The surf was crashing on the shore, and when she glanced down the beach, she could see a large area of rocks that secluded the beach from any other homes. Not that she could see any at the moment.

"What do you think?" Maka stopped next to her.

"It's so beautiful." She smiled over at him.

"I can't believe we're staying here."

"Well, not here." He smiled and then nodded. She followed his eyes and saw the dark roof of a house just up the rocky pathway. "Maka's guest house. We've got that one all to ourselves."

She couldn't have been more shocked and pleased if he'd told her they were moving there.

"It's a little hike, but the view…" He whistled.

"I've stocked the kitchen, but you're welcome to join us tomorrow night for dinner around seven," Maka said, setting her bags down on the coral driveway. "You can have use of the Jeep while you're here." He nodded and tossed the keys to Cole. "Your boards are where they always are." He nodded to the garage and then turned to her. "If you wish, I can give you lessons." His smile spread when he heard Cole mutter under his breath, "Or not."

She smiled and shook his hand. "Thank you." Then she bent down and picked up her luggage and followed Cole up the narrow stone path. Halfway up the hill, he stopped and nodded towards the water. "Dolphins."

She turned and watched the pod swimming close to the shoreline. From up here, the water looked so clear. There were large dark rocks directly below them, and she watched the waves crash for a minute before jogging to catch up with Cole.

When they made it to the top of the hill, Cole stopped and gave her a chance to look around. The guesthouse was a soft yellow cottage with a large front porch. Large brown flowerpots sat on every corner of the porch, and there was a dark brown wicker sofa covered with pillows and cushions. There was a small yard that led to the cliff, and she smiled when she saw the large hammock hanging between two palm trees.

"It's wonderful." She set her bag down on the porch and took a deep breath. He was right; the view was spectacular. The house was angled to look down the beach, so the entire North Shore was spread out in front of them. "This is his guesthouse?"

Cole chuckled. "Maka's family is pretty big. Hence the larger house down there." He nodded down the hill. "Besides, he likes to roll out of bed and into the water. Or so he always says." He chuckled as he picked up her bag and opened the unlocked sliding door.

"Has he always lived here?" She followed him into the house and stopped dead in her tracks. "Oh, my!" She blinked a few times and smiled.

"Like it?" He chuckled and set the bags down by the door.

"Wow." She shook her head. "This is his guesthouse?"

He nodded and took her hand. "Come on." The place had looked like a small cottage from the outside, but when they stepped in, the vaulted wood ceilings gave it a much bigger look. The house was one big room with the kitchen in the middle and a sitting area with two over-sized white leather sofas off to one side. An open eating area sat along a glass wall that overlooked a small swimming pool.

Cole gave a tour of the place. There were two smaller bedrooms towards the back, and the master bedroom over-looked the lawn and ocean. A king-sized four-poster bed sat facing the wall of windows.

"I'll say it again. This is his guesthouse?"

Cole chuckled. "Maka is always having guests. I've stayed here myself more than two dozen times." He fell back onto the bed and crossed his arms behind his head. "So, what do you want to do first?" he asked as he wiggled his eyebrows.

She smiled and walked slowly towards him. "I was

thinking about getting out of some of these clothes," she flirted.

"Oh?" His eyes heated as he watched her move closer.

She nodded slowly. "Mmm, stripping down," she sighed as she pulled her shirt up slowly.

"Yeah?" He leaned up on his elbows, his eyes watching her every move.

She stopped at the foot of the bed and pulled her shirt off all the way, exposing the cream-colored swimsuit she'd worn under her outfit. "Yeah, and then jumping in that pool." She chuckled as he pulled her down to the bed and covered her mouth with his.

Later—much later—they relaxed in the pool with drinks he'd made for her. She had to admit when he'd started to throw stuff together, she'd had her doubts. But after tasting the sweet drink, she was thinking of adding it to the Boardwalk's menu.

When they got hungry, Cole jumped out of the pool and disappeared into the house for a while. He came back out and put some chicken on the grill, then rushed back in and brought out a salad and more drinks.

"I could get used to being served like this." She held up her glass for him to refill as she lounged in one of the cushioned chairs.

He smiled at her. "My sister told me that you haven't taken a real vacation since you started working for her over three years ago."

She shrugged her shoulders. "I didn't really have any place to go. Besides, I'm too busy earning money to pay for Willow's college." She took another sip to shut herself up. She didn't want to think about her real life. Not while she was enjoying watching the sunset over the water.

He sat next to her and ran his hand over her hip. "What's she going to school for?"

She sighed. "This year?" She shook her head. "Marine biology."

His eyebrows shot up.

"Yeah, I know."

"What?" he asked, continuing to run his hand over her skin.

She shook her head. "It's just… A lot of people don't believe it's a good field of study."

"I'm not one of them. I make my living on the water. I know how important careers like that are." He sighed. "Actually, at one point, I was pretty interested in it myself."

Her eyebrows shot up. "Really?" She sat up a little and set her drink down.

"Sure," he smiled. "Before…"

She chuckled. "Before you started selling men's underwear?"

He smiled. "Hey, those things don't sell themselves."

She laughed. "So, when does this competition start?"

"Tomorrow morning."

"Shouldn't you be out practicing?"

He chuckled. "You don't really practice. Besides, since I've won the World Surf League championship for the last two years, I'm not really in this particular competition to win."

She narrowed her eyes at him. "I doubt that. You're in everything to win."

He chuckled and nodded. "Okay, maybe I am, but…" He sighed a little and looked off at the sun as it sank lower. "It just gets old, trying to keep up. I surf because I love it."

He glanced back at her. "You'll see. Tomorrow, I'll hit the water and have a dozen guys trying to knock me out."

"Literally?" She sat up a little and frowned.

He chuckled. "No, well…" He tilted his head. "There was this guy once in Australia…" He shook his head and got up to flip the chicken.

She followed him and stood next to him. "I thought surfing was dangerous enough on its own. Now you're telling me guys try to knock you off your board?"

He shook his head as he set the spatula down, took her hips in his hands, and pulled her close. "No, just one surfer in particular. I guess he didn't like that he came in second at WSL for two years."

"What's his name?"

He smiled. "Why? Are you going to go and beat him up?"

She chuckled. "Maybe."

He would never have guessed that "maybe" would mean so much to him. Sure, Deyon was an ass, but he would have paid anything to see Wendy tell the surfer off.

That night, after hanging out on the hammock after dinner, he carried Wendy into bed and spent as much time as he could, showing her how much her words had meant to him.

The next morning, when the sun came up, he was stoked. He woke early and, since Wendy was still sleeping, left her a note that he'd meet her down at the beach. He left directions on how to get to the competition, which was only a short walk down the beach from Maka's place.

After grabbing a quick bowl of cereal, a banana, and a bottled water, he went down to Maka's garage. His friend was already pulling the boards out.

"Morning." He smiled over at him. "Ready?"

Cole laughed. "I was born ready."

"Where's Ka makani `olu `olu?"

"Sleeping in." He frowned at his friend's nickname for Wendy, and then it dawned on him. "Oh, I get it. Wind… Wendy…" He shook his head and chuckled.

Maka just looked at him like he was crazy.

"Sorry, I guess I was a little jet-lagged yesterday." He picked out his board for the day, and Maka grabbed his backup board.

By the time they made it down the beach, there was a light trail of sweat dripping down his bare back. He was aching to get into the water, especially after seeing the waves kicking up.

"Look." Maka nodded towards the shore. "Your friend."

Cole glanced in the direction and groaned. Deyon was walking towards them, a hot blonde on either arm.

"Maka." He nodded towards Maka, then stopped right in front of them and looked at Cole. "Cole." Just the way the man said his name set off his nerves.

"Deyon." He held out his hand, only for it to be ignored, like usual.

"I didn't think you were going to make it, what with all your injuries." He chuckled.

"Injuries?" he asked.

"Didn't you crash your bicycle?" The man's English

wasn't very good, but Cole knew he'd used the word bicycle instead of a motorcycle on purpose.

Cole chuckled. "That was a while ago. Since then I've won the RCP and the ASP." He smiled and set his surfboard down.

"Yeah, I heard about that." He chuckled. "If you call those competitions." He nodded in Maka's direction then walked off before Cole could say anything else.

"That man's an ass," Maka said, causing Cole to laugh. He'd never heard his friend use the English version of the term before, always the Hawaiian, which sounded less harsh. "What?" Maka turned to him. "He is."

"True. I guess I'd better go check in." He nodded towards the line that was quickly growing.

"You go sign in; I'll stay here and wax." Maka sat in the sand and started working on Cole's surfboards.

Cole walked over to the check-in table and chatted with a few friends. Most of the surfers he'd seen over the years were pretty cool. Most of them looked out for one another if the occasion called for it. There was always an underlying competition, but it was an honest sport. At least in Cole's mind.

There was a group of women that seemed to follow the circuit, and then there were the surfer chicks, as they were called. Some of them scared the hell out of Cole. He would be the last to admit it, but he wondered how the hell he was supposed to compete against a girl that could if she wanted to, do a backbend on a surfboard. Not that he'd seen anything like that in person, but...

His thoughts were broken when a cool hand reached up and ran down his back. Turning around, he smiled at Carly.

"Hey." He leaned in and placed a kiss on her cheek. Carly was one of the followers. He'd never seen the woman step foot in the water, even though she always wore a stark white bikini, which she filled out very nicely.

"Hi, I was hoping you'd be here." She leaned a little towards him. He'd known her for almost as long as he'd been on the circuit. She was a good ten years older than him and turned every head on the beach.

"Oh?" He moved up in the line and saw that there were only two people now in front of him.

"Yes, I haven't seen you since the Gold Coast," she purred. "I was hoping that maybe we could see one another."

With her chest pressing up against his, he fully understood her meaning. She'd shown interest in him a few times, but nothing as blatant as this before.

"Uh, I'm with someone," he blurted out, taking her hands in his and removing them from his waist, where they were dangerously traveling lower.

"Oh?" She blinked and then looked around.

"She's still sleeping, but she'll be along later." He moved farther away from her and smiled. "I'll talk with you later," he said, just as it was his turn to step up to the table. He felt a surge of relief flood through him when she frowned and walked away.

A few months ago, he would have been all over that. No matter how empty it would have made him feel. He was so thankful that streak of his life was over.

After checking in and stopping almost a dozen times to chat with other friends, he made his way back to Maka. He smiled when he saw Wendy sitting next to him in the sand.

She'd brought a portable beach chair and a cooler. "I

brought lunches." She smiled up at him as he leaned down and placed a kiss on her lips.

"Hmm, and dessert," he whispered against her lips. She chuckled as he sat next to her in the sand. "I'm all checked in."

"Good." She blinked a few times and he watched her bite her bottom lip. "Maka was just telling me about Carly." She nodded towards the blonde, who was glancing his way.

"Oh?" He felt his stomach flip a little.

"Yeah." She sighed. "She sure looked glued to you."

He chuckled. "Don't worry, she's not my type." He took her hand in his and brought it up to his lips. He watched her eyebrows shoot up in question.

"Really, because I seem to remember—"

"Wendy." He smiled as he interrupted her. "I didn't spend last night with Carly, and I don't want to spend tonight or the next with anyone other than you."

She frowned a little and then glanced down at their joined hands. "It's just so hard to…" She sighed.

"Hey, I guess we haven't talked about…" Just then Maka stood up and walked over to them.

"Ready?" He nodded towards the shore.

"Yeah, I guess I'd better get out there and show these guys how to surf." He smiled and looked down at Wendy. "Later." He waited until she nodded then grabbed his board and headed out.

CHAPTER 13

The next few hours were complete hell for Wendy. Every time Cole disappeared below a wave, her heart skipped. She watched in amazement as he rode each wave with ease, weaving in and out of the other surfers or the photographers that littered the water.

Since her eyes were glued to Cole, she didn't see the big wipe-out that had broken another surfer's board. He'd been carried out of the surf in a neck brace.

"He's young," Maka said, sitting beside her in the sand.

Since they'd been there, many people had stopped by to talk to Maka. Some he chatted with, other's he'd just nod his head at and they would go on their way.

"You seem to know a lot of people." She propped her elbows on her knees as her eyes zeroed back in on Cole.

"I've been surfing since I was five." He smiled at her. "Most come and go, but those who stick around know my name."

She smiled. "I think the whole world knows your name."

He chuckled. "Don't tell that to my kids."

Her eyebrows shot up. "You have kids?"

He laughed and then pointed to another surfer. "My son, Makaha. This is his tenth competition." He smiled. "My daughter, Maka Nani goes to the university next year."

"Are they both named after you?" She chuckled and leaned back.

He smiled. "My actual name is Maka Koa, fierce one."

"Oh, yes." She laughed. "I can see it now. You're so fierce."

He smiled. "Again, don't tell that to my kids."

"How did you meet Cole?"

Maka laughed. "I saw him surf years ago and approached him after."

She tilted her head in question.

"If you haven't noticed, a lot of surfers approach me and ask that I train or teach them."

She nodded. Over a dozen had already done so that day. All of which he'd declined.

"I have only approached two myself."

She let that sink in. "Who was the second one?"

He smiled and then nodded towards a surfer in blue shorts. "Deyon Colston."

"Is he any good?"

He chuckled. "Second best in the world." His eyes traveled over to where Cole was swimming out. "I still regret it."

"Oh?" She turned a little towards him and watched him nod.

"He has a hole, here…" He tapped his chest over his heart.

Wendy's eyes moved back over to the surfer and watched him for a few minutes. He was a powerful surfer, but she watched as he repetitively came too close to the heads of swimmers or cameramen.

"Is that the guy who knocked Cole off his board." She frowned as she watched the man jump off his board into the water near Cole.

Maka glanced at her and then burst out laughing. "Oh, I do like you Ka makani `olu `olu."

She smiled. "Thanks. I like you too."

She thought Cole would come in for lunch, but instead, he just drank some water and headed right back out to the water. She didn't know how they were being judged, or for that matter, who was doing the judging.

She knew the competition lasted two more days, but Maka told her that Cole would just have one more day to compete. By the time Cole called it quits for the day, she was tired herself and could only imagine what he must feel like. He must be exhausted and extremely hungry.

When Cole walked up to her, he looked like he was energized.

"How do you do it?" She shook her head as he jogged next to her in the sand.

He chuckled. "It's like having my batteries recharged." He smiled over at her. "Let's go out tonight. There's this little place not too far from here.

She nodded. "I'll need a shower first."

He smiled and stepped closer to her, and even with the large surfboard between them, she felt his heat. "I'll need one too."

She swallowed hard and nodded slowly.

Cole sat across from Wendy and couldn't take his eyes off of her. She was wearing a white cotton dress, which hugged her curves beautifully. She had large dangling silver hoops in her ears and she'd left her hair down, flowing around her face.

They sat at the Hukilau Cafe, one of his favorite hole-in-the-wall kind of places and ate some of the best burgers in the world.

"I've never had eggs on a burger before." She frowned down at the burger.

He smiled. "Once you try it, you'll never eat a burger without one again."

She nodded, then picked up the large thing and tried to shove it into her mouth. He watched and felt his own mouthwatering just watching her.

After taking a bite, she closed her eyes and sighed as she chewed. "Wow," she said after taking a drink of her soda. "Incredible."

He chuckled and picked up his own burger. "Told you." She nodded as she took another bite.

"So, how does this competition thing work? I mean, I didn't see any judges."

"Depends on the competition. Something like this one, we're usually judged on speed, style and the power of the ride and wave. Since this is a big wave competition, the bigger the wave and ride, the higher the points." He took another bite of his burger.

He loved talking about surfing, so for the next half

hour, he told her all the ins and outs of his trade. The fact that she hung on his every word was not only a happy surprise but exciting. Most of the women he'd been involved with before didn't like it when he talked shop. In fact, they all tried to steer the conversation towards his modeling career and which celebrities he'd met.

"So, that's how it's decided who gets to ride the wave." He finished up the conversation as he slapped down some cash on the table to pay for their meal. "Now, I know this great place to get ice cream."

She laughed and followed him as he took her hand and led her outside. "I like this side of you." She smiled as he helped her into the Jeep.

"Oh?" He turned and looked at her as she nodded.

"Yes, you seem less… hindered."

He thought about it as he walked around and jumped behind the wheel. "I guess I feel that way in the water." He shrugged his shoulders as he pulled out of the parking lot and headed towards Angel's Ice Cream shop a couple miles away. "It's the way you are… behind the bar." He glanced at her and saw that she was frowning. "Come on, don't try to deny it." He smiled. "You enjoy your job."

She nodded. "Yeah, but…" She glanced towards him. "I never really thought of it as what I was meant to do. I mean, I have other dreams."

He glanced at her and waited. When she didn't finish, he prodded. "Like?"

She chuckled. "I don't know."

He laughed. "Join the club."

"I guess my first dream is to see my sister graduate school." He nodded. "My second is to pay off her school." She chuckled again.

"With her help," he suggested.

"Oh, of course." She didn't sound very convincing.

"What is it you're not telling me?" He pulled into the parking lot of the ice cream place and stopped, and then he turned towards her and waited.

"Nothing." She shook her head and then sighed. "Okay, so she might not know that I'm paying for her school. Exactly."

He blinked. "Who, exactly, does she think is paying for her school?"

She sighed. "A trust fund that dad set up for her."

"Why would she think that?"

"Because that's what I told her a year ago when she told me she didn't want to be a burden and had decided to get a job instead of going to school." She leaned her head back and sighed.

He chuckled. "The things we'll do for our siblings." He took her hand and brought it to his lips. He loved watching her eyes go soft when he kissed her hand. "Willow sounds like a smart girl. I'm sure by now she's figured it out."

Wendy nodded and smiled. "Now, you promised me some ice cream?" He laughed.

The next day's competition was even rougher. The waves were better than the day before, and Maka looked like he'd rather be out riding them than sitting in the sand next to her.

"Why don't you compete anymore?" she asked,

watching Cole take his turn down a particularly large wave.

"I retired almost fifteen years ago," he said.

She chuckled. "I bet that was hard, sitting out, just watching."

He shrugged his shoulder. "It's no longer my time. I'm a kumu now." He glanced at her. "Teacher. I pick the surfers I want to teach, around ten a year, and that satisfies me."

She sighed. "I suppose." She leaned on her knees and watched Cole finish his ride. "I doubt Cole will ever get this out of his system."

Maka tilted his head a little. "You'd be surprised. One day, he will ride a wave and decide that it's not enough. That he's still missing something."

"What were you missing?"

He smiled and nodded to where his daughter sat, watching her brother. "Them. I was traveling too much. Before I knew it, Nani had learned to walk without my help." He frowned a little. "So, I retired and started taking on students, so I could be home with my family." He turned and smiled at her. "Best decision I've ever made."

She smiled back at him. "So, when will we know who won?" She glanced around.

"In a few hours. Tomorrow's competition is a different division and is judged separately."

She bit her lip and glanced around. Today she could easily spot the judges, sitting or standing around the beach with their clipboards. Listening to Cole explain the rules last night over dinner really helped her understand the sport.

Today she watched every competitor for their style and

speed. So far today, there had been three very large, impressive waves, and Cole had been lucky enough to catch one of them. She frowned as she watched Deyon take another impressive ride down a larger wave.

"Is Deyon going to be a problem for Cole?"

Maka nodded a little. "He always is."

She bit her bottom lip as she watched Deyon ride the curve of a big wave. Near the base of the wave, he lost his balance and wiped out. She heard the whole beach gasp as they watched one of the best riders tumble in the surf.

"But, it appears, not anymore," Maka said under his breath.

CHAPTER 14

"We're having dinner down at Maka's tonight," Cole said as they walked back up to their little house on the cliff, his very large trophy tucked under his arm.

"Sounds good. We should celebrate." She smiled and nodded towards his first-place prize. It was a large wood carving of a surfboard, and Cole held onto it like it was made of glass.

He chuckled. "Sounds more than good. Have you ever been to a luau before?"

She stopped and turned around to look down at him. "A real luau?" When he nodded, she shook her head no. "I've always wanted to go to one."

"Well, here's your chance." He chuckled.

"I can't remember if I bought anything festive to wear." She frowned and thought about it.

He laughed. "I'm sure that whatever you wear tonight will be perfect." He moved closer to her and kissed her on her lips.

At seven o'clock that evening, they walked back down the pathway. Wendy was shocked to see the transformation of the beach in front of Maka's house. Long tables full of food lined the grass area, while smaller ones sat around in the soft sand. There were three hula dancers shaking their grass skirts as men played the drums while sitting in the sand.

There were at least forty other people gathered around, enjoying themselves.

"Here, I'll introduce you to a few people." He took her hand and pulled her towards the crowd. When she noticed that most of the women were wearing shorts and bikini tops, she glanced down at her blue sundress and felt over-dressed.

Cole walked her past a table where a large roasted pig lay spread out with pineapples and flowers all around him. The food smelled so good, she felt her stomach growl.

"First, can we eat?" She tugged on his hand. He smiled. "We'll wait for Maka; then we'll eat." He nodded to where Maka sat in a high-backed chair. He had a large wreath of grass on top of his head and a green skirt wrapped around his hips. A short, dark-haired woman sat next to him in a smaller chair. Her head was circled in flowers, and her beautiful floral dress made Wendy wish she had had time to go shopping on the island before tonight.

She glanced at all the food as Cole tugged her along to meet several other people he knew. She was too hungry to focus on what their names were or what they did.

Finally, after the sun had gone down, a young woman approached them. She was wearing a simple Hawaiian dress and had a wreath of flowers in her long dark hair.

"My father wishes you to sit next to him," she said.

Cole smiled. "We'd be honored." They followed her to the main table where Maka and his wife sat.

"This is my mother, Kanunu." She smiled, and Wendy could see where the young woman got her pretty smile. Other than that, she looked just like her father. "Please." She motioned for them to sit.

When they sat, Maka stood up and clapped his hands and the music and dancing stopped. Everyone took their seats and listened as he spoke about good friends, good waves, and great food. When he sat back down, the music started up again as everyone took turns filling their plates.

As the last people were seated, the drums began to beat faster as four male fire dancers walked into the sand and lit their batons on fire. Wendy had never seen anything like it before and was so engrossed in watching, she forgot about her hunger.

"Impressive, aren't they?" Maka's wife leaned closer to her.

"Very." She smiled over at the other woman.

"That is our Makaha." She nodded to the lead dancer as she smiled.

"Impressive." She clapped as he sprayed a big ball of fire from his mouth, which ended the show.

Once the male dancers finished, the conversation started back up as everyone ate. Wendy went back to slating her hunger as she listened to Cole and Maka talk about the day's competition.

A large bonfire was lit in the sand and after everyone had stuffed themselves, some people sat on blankets in the sand around the fire.

"Want to go for a walk?" Cole asked, holding out his

hand. Smiling, she reached up and took it, letting him pull her along.

"So, what did you think?" he asked after a while, nodding back towards the party.

She sighed. "It's all so wonderful." She wrapped her arm through his as she listened to the waves crash along the rocks. "I can't believe you get to do this for a living."

He chuckled. "Beats standing in my underwear in a cold room as someone snaps pictures."

She smiled. "So, why do you do it?"

He shrugged his shoulders as they stopped near the edge of the water. The sounds and lights from the party were far down the beach, so all she could hear was the steady sound of the waves.

"To help my family out."

She frowned a little. "I don't understand."

He tugged on her arm until they sat in the soft sand, side by side. "Dad and Julie have been struggling lately. I kick a chunk over to help pay for things, as well as helping Roman out with Spring Haven."

"I know about everyone kicking in for the home for kids, but Cassey told me Julie's been renting out some rooms."

He shrugged. "Sure, she does that during the season."

"What about your future?" She turned a little towards him, wondering what he had planned for himself.

Cole listened to her words and could no longer deny that he'd been asking himself the same question since he'd kissed her.

"I have some ideas tucked away." He thought about his accounts and for the first time ever, imagined buying a house along the shore where he could settle down. He'd never cared about owning things. He had a used truck he drove when he was in town, his surfboards, and the clothes on his back. Oh, and his bike. He frowned, thinking about how he'd just abandoned it to the junkyard. Sure, he could have spent the insurance money to fix it up or buy a new one, but so far, he hadn't. Roman had teased him that he kept putting it off because he was afraid of getting back on the thing.

"Good." She sighed and leaned back against his shoulder.

"We haven't talked about…" He sighed and closed his eyes as he took in her soft scent. "Us."

She chuckled. "Cole, I'm not asking for commitments." She glanced up at him and then buried her fingers into his hair, pulling him closer to her.

"Wendy…" It was on the tip of his tongue to tell her exactly how he felt, but then she was kissing him, and his body demanded more of her. His hands sunk into her hair as he fell backward with her on top.

Her sweet body pushed against his; every inch of her was pressed next to him. His hands traveled down her sides until he felt her soft skin and he knew he needed more. Running his hands up her legs, he hiked the skirt of her dress up until he could feel her moan next to his mouth.

"I want you," he said between kisses. "Here…" He hooked a finger under the silky bottoms she was wearing until he could feel her slick heat, waiting for him. "Now."

She smiled and nodded against his lips. Then she put

her hands on his chest and sat up, slowly moving her skirt up over her thighs. His hands moved to her arms and gripped her as she steadied herself above him. "Touch me," she whispered.

His fingers brushed the sides of her breasts and her head rolled back on a moan. Pulling the spaghetti strap down, he ran his fingers over the edge of the material and her breath hitched. Leaning up, he ran his tongue over the swell of her breast and released a moan of his own.

"Perfect." He gently nudged the straps down her shoulders until she was freed. Then his mouth covered her as her nails dug into his shoulders.

"Cole," she moaned, "I want…"

He nodded, knowing exactly what she wanted. Pulling out a condom, he yanked down his shorts and a few seconds later, she slid slowly down his length. He leaned back in the sand as she hovered over him, taking what she wanted and giving him what he needed.

When they walked back to their cabin, the party was just dying down. The fire was only embers as a few guests hung around.

"I hope it's okay, but I have a full day of adventurous things planned for us tomorrow," he said as they walked into the house.

She nodded, and he could tell that she was holding back a yawn. "Like?"

He smiled. "I want to surprise you." He took her hand and walked towards the bedroom. "But, I will tell you this… you'll need your sleep tonight." He chuckled as she yawned.

He loved lying in the bed, holding her close to his body as she slept. He couldn't believe how much she had come to mean to him. It was like he couldn't breathe without her nearby.

He'd lied to her earlier. The truth was, he had no clue what he wanted for his future, other than making sure she was in it. At one point, he'd thought of moving to the West Coast and opening a surf school but being that far from his family would kill him. Then he'd thought he would just work for his brothers. But after a few days of building, he had quickly decided he was too much of a free spirit to be tied to a job where you had to wear steel-toed boots every day.

Sighing, he smiled when Wendy snuggled closer to his chest. One thing was perfectly clear—whatever he did decide on, he would make sure she was right there next to him.

The next morning, he woke up just as the sun was rising. When he moved to wake Wendy, he was shocked to find her side of the bed was empty.

He heard her moving around in the kitchen and relaxed. After showering, he walked into the big room and smiled. She was standing at the stove, wearing only his T-shirt and cooking.

"This is a sight." He walked over and leaned on the counter next to her.

She smiled at him. "I figured if we are going to have a full day of adventure, we need a good start."

"Perfect. Can I help?" he asked, watching her flip a pancake.

She shook her head no. "I've got everything under control." She nodded towards the table area. It was already set and there was a large bowl of eggs and a plate of bacon. Fresh flowers sat in a vase in the middle of it all.

"You woke up pretty early today." He smiled.

"I guess I'm just excited." She scooped a pancake onto a plate that was already stacked with them.

"That's the last." She nodded and walked over to set the plate on the table with the rest of the food. "Orange juice?"

He smiled and walked over to her, only stopping when she was wrapped in his arms. "Thank you." He kissed her.

"For?"

"Breakfast. Coming with me on this trip. Everything." He kissed her in between each statement.

She wrapped her arms around his shoulders and smiled. "You." Kiss. "Are." Another kiss. "Welcome." This last kiss lasted longer, and his blood started to heat.

When he started walking her back towards the bedroom, she laughed and pulled away.

"Oh, no, you don't. My idea of a day filled with adventure is not spending it in that bedroom."

He chuckled. "Are you sure?"

She nodded, but he thought he saw her swallow hard.

endy held onto the handles in the Jeep as it bounced up the bumpiest lane she'd ever seen.

"Where did you say we were going?" She glanced over at Cole, who looked like he was enjoying the back roads a little too much.

"I didn't." He kept his eyes glued to the pathway.

"Any hints?"

He chuckled and shook his head.

They had driven to the other side of the island, and she had enjoyed seeing more of the land and shore as he drove along. He'd told her to wear her swimsuit, shorts, and a T-shirt, but had also told her to put on sturdy shoes. She'd gone with her running shoes since she hadn't brought hiking boots.

The Jeep finally came to a stop in a small parking area where there were a few other off-road vehicles parked.

"Well?" He turned to her. "Are you ready?" She

nodded as he grabbed a backpack from the back seat of the Jeep.

She followed him towards a small path, and then they walked through some tall trees in silence for a while. "How did you find this place?" she asked, a little winded as she jogged to keep up with him. When he turned around, he frowned and held out a water bottle.

"Sorry, I didn't know I was going too fast."

"You weren't." She thought about taking up jogging when they got back home.

He smiled. "Maka brought me here the first time I visited. Not many tourists know about this place. It's kind of a locals-only thing." She took a drink of water.

"It's lovely." She handed the bottle back to him.

"Wait until we get where we are going." He took a swig of the water and then started walking again, this time much more slowly.

It took almost forty minutes before they came to a clearing. When Cole stopped, she thought he was taking another break, for her sake. Since the first stop, he'd taken one every ten minutes. When she moved next to him, her breath hitched.

A two-story waterfall sat directly in front of them, and there was a small pool of crystal clear water below it. The area was surrounded by trees, giving it a completely secluded feeling. She could see a few other people bathing in the water below and instantly wanted to jump in.

"It's beautiful." She reached over and took his hand as he smiled down at her.

"Come on, let's go cool off." He tugged her hand as she laughed.

They spent a few hours enjoying the cool water and

then sat near the edge of the water and ate the sandwiches he'd made for them. When they started to hike back down, she felt completely rejuvenated.

"Stop one is out of the way," he said when they made it back to the Jeep.

"One?" She smiled as he nodded.

"Next stop, coming up."

They drove into town and he pulled into a small gas station where there were over a dozen mopeds parked.

"I'll be right back." He smiled and quickly disappeared. When he came back out, he was jiggling a set of keys. "Do you want to drive or shall I?"

"Drive what?" She frowned a little. When he nodded towards the mopeds, she laughed as she jumped out of the Jeep. "I will." She grabbed the keys from him.

"I thought you would." He smiled. "Come on, we have this one." He walked over to a green one and patted the seat.

"Where to?" she asked, sitting down and holding on as he jumped on behind her.

"You're driving." He laughed.

She reached behind her and tied her hair up, then leaned down to turn the bike on. "I've never driven one of these before." She frowned.

"Gas, brakes, gears." He showed her each step by covering her hand with his. "It's easy." She nodded and slowly made her way out of the parking lot.

Less than an hour later, she was a pro at it. "The second I get home, I'm buying one of these," she said over the sound of the engine. She'd driven them through town and was enjoying the beachfront roads.

"Someday I might get you on my hog," he said,

causing her to stiffen a little at the thought of something bigger.

"I doubt it." She chuckled.

"Pull in here." He pointed to a small shop area on the side of the beach way.

When she stood up, she felt her legs shake a little from the excitement. "That was fun." She smiled and watched him make sure the kickstand was down.

"Wait until I get a chance to drive." He laughed as they walked towards the shop. "I love this place." He took her hand and walked her over to the counter. "They have these cute little shells." He nodded towards a glass case.

The "cute little shells" happened to be made from silver and gold and were sprinkled with diamond dust. She was totally shocked when he bought her a beautiful silver necklace with small black mussel shells made into a heart shape.

She touched it lightly as she got on the back of the bike. When he took off out of the driveway, her arms went around him quickly, and she held on tightly as he zipped down the open road. She had to admit, she really did enjoy the speed and the wind.

They weren't going too fast—the bike topped out at forty-five miles per hour—but since she doubted she'd gotten the thing over twenty, it was a nice change to have the cool breeze hit her face.

They rode in silence for a while, and then he pulled into a small parking area near the edge of the beach. There was another small shack, and when she got off the bike, the sweet smells of cooking meat hit her, making her stomach growl loudly.

Cole chuckled. "My thoughts exactly."

The place looked like nothing more than a small trailer parked on the side of the road with a few picnic benches out front. But when Cole walked her around back, she realized how wrong she was. On the sand, nestled between the small hut and the water, was a larger dining area in the sand. There was a small stage where hula dancers swayed to a beat. More picnic tables spread out on the beach, and they were almost completely filled with people.

They found an empty table near the edge of the water and watched the show for a while before someone delivered a large plate of food. No one had taken their order or asked them what they wanted; they had just delivered the food. It was delicious.

"They cook like this once a month." He smiled over at her.

"It's wonderful." She took another bite of the meat. "I would have never thought that this was a restaurant."

He chuckled. "It's not."

She frowned over at him. "What do you mean?"

"It's owned by a family." He nodded towards the stage. "Mother, daughters." Then he nodded towards the man who'd delivered the food. "Brothers and father over there cooking. They never charge anyone."

She looked over to where an older man stood, carving the meat from a large pig.

"How do they make a living?" She glanced around and frowned.

He smiled. "Tips mostly, but this is their way of saying thank you to the Islanders and tourists for providing for their family."

They watched the show the family put on and clapped when it was all over. When they walked away, she saw

Cole drop cash into their donation bucket. She wished she'd brought her purse, so she could give them some money as well.

"We'd better get the bike back. It's getting late." He walked her back to the parking lot and helped her on. He smiled over his shoulder at her as they left the parking area. "Hang on to me."

The entire trip back to the Jeep, those words played over and over in her mind, and she decided she didn't want to ever let him go. Not after today.

The next day Cole took her surfing. It was fun to watch her try new things. It took her a while, but she finally mastered it with his help. He was happily surprised when she started to easily get up on the board next to him.

Then he decided to try something new and walked up to get Maka's longboard from the garage.

"This should be fun." He smiled as they paddled the big board out.

"Have you ever done this before?" she asked.

He chuckled. "No, but I've seen it done." He smiled over at her and turned the board around, setting up for a ride. "Just follow my lead." He started paddling when he saw the opportunity. She followed along. When he stood, she stood up in front of him. His hands went to her hips for just a moment and then they fell.

When she surfaced, she was laughing. "You knocked me off balance." She splashed water in his face. "Let's try that again."

He nodded, and they paddled out once more. This time,

instead of touching her hips right away, he stood behind her as they both gained their balance.

When he felt that they were balanced, he took her hips in his hands and spun her around. He shocked her by reaching down and taking her legs and arms and pulling her up over his head smoothly. She easily went with him and laughed as she threw one leg up in the air.

She was laughing and having a great time until he lost his balance and tossed her into the wave, falling after her.

"Let's do that again. This time, I'll sit on your shoulders," she said after she swam back to him.

He laughed and shook his head. "It's worth trying."

They paddled out and waited until the right wave came. This time when she got up on his shoulders, she surprised him by glancing down at him and saying, "Help me stand up."

He reached up and took her hands while keeping balanced. She placed her feet carefully on his shoulders and stood up as she held onto his hands.

Then he tugged on her hands and she sat back down. When he felt the wave dying, he flipped her over his shoulders and tucked her next to him as they hit the water.

His lips covered hers when they surfaced. "I haven't had this much fun in years." She smiled at him. "What else can we do?" He laughed.

"It depends on how flexible you are and how willing you are to let me toss you around."

She smiled. "I trust you."

They spent over two hours playing in the surf. They got to the point where he could hold her with one hand as she posed above him.

He had to admit, they were a pretty good team.

When they carried the board back up to the beach, Maka was sitting there with his daughter.

"You two should enter the tandem competitions next year," Nani said.

Cole looked to Maka, who nodded. "With some work, you could place."

He laughed. "I'm game if Wendy will go along with it."

She sat in the sand and laughed. Then she surprised him by smiling and saying, "Sounds fun."

endy hated to say goodbye to Hawaii. She even felt sad saying goodbye to Maka and his family. But the moment the plane took off, she had to admit that the vacation had worn her out.

Not only had surfing yesterday made her sore, she had a few bruises on her body to go along with the aches. Cole sat beside her in first class, fast asleep. Her mind didn't shut down until halfway through the flight.

Then she was blinking as Cole shook her awake. "We're landing." He smiled. "Two more flights to go and we're home."

Just the sound of it made her heartache. Her entire life she'd felt like she was missing something in life by not traveling. Now, however, she knew that the best part of a trip was returning home.

"I bet you can't wait to get back to work," he joked as they boarded their second flight.

"Right." She rolled her eyes and took her seat. "What

about you? What are your plans?" She held her breath for his answer.

"I'm not sure. I have a few things lined up." He frowned. "Tracking down my brother might just be one of them."

"Have you heard from Roman?"

He shook his head. "Not since the last call."

"I'm sure he's okay." She took his hand.

He chuckled. "You wouldn't say that if you'd seen him when he left."

"Why?" She frowned, instantly getting worried.

He shook his head and sighed. "There was something off about him."

"Like?"

He looked at her. "He hadn't cut his hair for weeks, he was growing a beard, and..." He cringed. "He looked like me."

She chuckled. "Is that so bad?"

He shook his head and glanced down at himself. He was wearing old blue surf shorts, a T-shirt that he'd probably had since high school, and flip-flops that had seen better days. "Not for me, but Roman..."

She thought about how his brother had always looked put together. Even when he spent a day at the beach, he looked like he could have just stepped off a magazine cover.

"Okay, now you're freaking me out."

He chuckled. "Yeah, I know." He squeezed her hand.

"Did he tell you where he was really going?"

He shook his head no. "Just that he wasn't leaving the state."

She chewed her bottom lip. "Have you tracked his phone?"

He blinked. "You can do that?"

She laughed and nodded. "Are you on the same plan as he is?"

He nodded. "We all are on the family plan."

She held out her hand. "Give me your phone."

She set up the provider app that would show him where his brother was. When it finally came up, she handed the phone back to him.

"There, he's on Dog Island." She pointed to the red dot.

"Dog?" He looked down at the screen. "That's near Carrabelle. That's only three hours from home." He frowned and then set his phone down.

"So, I guess I know what you'll be doing this week." She smiled as he nodded.

"Have you texted him?"

He nodded again. "He hasn't answered since before we left for Hawaii."

"I'm sure he has his reasons."

"Yeah, he's an idiot." She chuckled and tugged on his hand until he looked at her.

"Willow is like that. She never responds to my messages. Then, when we have plans, she always flakes or forgets. We were supposed to go…" She dropped off and gasped. "Oh my god!" She closed her eyes and rested her head back.

"What?" He leaned towards her. "What's wrong?"

"The concert," she whispered, feeling a little light-headed. Reaching into her bag, she pulled out her phone and texted Willow quickly as Cole watched.

Her sister didn't respond, which was nothing new.

"I can't believe I forgot." She shook her head. "I'm a terrible sister."

He tugged on her hand until she looked at him. "Talk to me."

She sighed. "I was so upset that she'd flaked the last time we were supposed to spend the weekend together, and then I pull something like this."

"What?" he asked again.

"We were going to go to the Summer Bash concert at the Hang Out. It was yesterday, and I totally forgot."

"I'm sure she'll understand."

She closed her eyes and felt a sinking feeling start to overtake her. "Yeah, I know you're right. But I should have been there."

"Did you at least tell her you were going to Hawaii?"

She glared at him. "Of course, I did."

He chuckled. "Then you're a better sibling than my brother." He smiled. "I'm sure she understands that you were excited for the trip and forgot the concert. At least tell me she had her ticket."

She nodded. "She had both of ours."

"See." He smiled. "Then she probably took her boyfriend."

At the mention of Jake, she cringed again and shook her head. "No, Jake left a few days ago for basic, and I wasn't there to help her get over his leaving."

He sighed. "Wendy, you can't shelter your sister from everything."

She glanced at him. "I know." She frowned, thinking about it. "I don't."

His eyebrows shot up. "So, then you'll tell her you've been paying her tuition?"

She sighed and thought about it. "Yes, fine."

He chuckled. "It's for the best."

She knew that and was determined to follow through.

When she parked her Jeep in front of her condo, she felt a wave of happiness overcome her. She'd dropped Cole off at his apartment, even though he'd wanted to come back to her place with her. She had needed some time alone. Besides, it was well after midnight and all she wanted now was a shower and sleep.

When she walked in, there were four messages on her machine. The first two were hang-ups, the third was from Willow.

"Hey, I hope you're having a good time on your trip. I didn't want to bug you on your cell phone, but I wanted to let you know that I'm quitting school and following Jake to basic training. When you get home, I'll most likely be gone. So, anyway, I'll talk to you later."

Wendy felt the room spin, so she quickly sat down and put her head between her knees. Then, through the ringing in her ears, she heard the last message and quickly rushed to rewind it and play it again.

Wendy's voice sounded muffled and she thought she heard her sniff. *"Hey... I didn't go. Jake's been cheating on me. He has a kid! He's lied to me. I guess I'm just calling to let you know that I'm back home. Bye."*

Wendy rushed over and picked up her phone and dialed her sister's number. On the third ring, Willow answered.

"Hello?"

"Hey, are you okay?" Wendy asked, holding the phone tight to her ear.

"Yeah." Silence.

"I'm sorry about Jake." She heard sniffling.

"It's okay. He's an ass."

Wendy chuckled and smiled. "Most men are. I'm sorry I missed the concert."

"It's okay. I took Micayla." She sighed, and Wendy could hear her sister blow her nose. "We met some boys."

Wendy laughed. "Of course, you did." Wendy sighed. "So, you're back at school Monday?"

Willow sighed. "Yeah, I'll go back."

Wendy decided it was now or never. "I don't know if you knew this or not…"

Willow sighed. "Wendy? I'm really tired."

"Yeah." She sighed and listened to her sister breathe for a while.

"I've known you're paying for my college from the start," Willow broke in.

"How?" Wendy tucked her feet under her and leaned back on the sofa.

Willow laughed. "The first day, they handed me a receipt for my first semester. I plan on paying you back."

Wendy smiled. "You don't have…"

"Wendy," she broke in. "Thank you."

The next day Wendy walked into work with a huge smile on her face. She'd had the best conversation with her sister since… well… ever.

It was so nice to feel that weight lifted from her shoulders that it took her a while to realize the place was dead.

She walked over to the bar, where Alan was leaning against the counter, facing away from the door.

"Hey, what's up?" Upon hearing her voice, he spun around and smiled at her.

"Well, look who's back from paradise."

"Paradise is here." She smiled and hugged him.

"Not for long," he said and then nodded towards the television. "Hurricanes a-comin."

"Oh, yeah?" She'd ridden out some rough ones and since she'd been born and raised on the gulf, she knew which ones to flee and which ones to ride out. "Bad one?"

"Naw, nothing we haven't seen before." He smiled and bumped her hip and then sighed. "But, of course, that means it will be dead around here until it passes."

"Yeah." She bit her bottom lip. She was really hoping to make up some of that money she'd spent in Hawaii.

"Look on the bright side." Alan chuckled. "At least we get to have another hurricane party."

CHAPTER 17

Cole glanced down at the red dot on his phone and cursed. He'd been sitting outside of the small house for almost an hour. Still, when he rang the door, no one answered, least of all his brother.

The most he could tell was that the place was well kept. The metal roof looked fairly new and the siding was freshly painted a light teal. Even the white picket fence out front was spotless. He wondered whose house it was, and why his brother's cell phone would be left there, unattended.

Roman never went anywhere without his phone. Then he remembered the day his brother had left and felt a sick feeling wash over him, causing him to curse once more.

Just then, a dark-haired kid rode his bike up to the house. When the kid dumped his bike in the front yard, Cole jumped from the truck and rushed over.

"Hey," he called out, and the boy turned around quickly and glared at him.

"Hey," he finally said when he realized Cole wasn't going to cross the fence line.

"Do you know Roman Grayton?" he called out.

The kid squinted his eyes at him, and Cole felt a wave of deja vu hit him. Then the kid put his hand up and blocked out the sun. "Yeah."

Cole sighed. "Is he staying here?"

The kid shrugged his shoulders. "Maybe. Why?"

"He's my brother and I'm looking for him."

"He's down at the docks," the kid said, and then he turned to go into the house.

"Which docks?" he called out, but the kid was already inside. Cole smiled when he heard the locks click behind him. Smart kid.

The docks were less than three blocks away, but he drove since he didn't know exactly where he'd end up. He spotted his brother's car right away since there were only two large buildings along the road.

Pulling in next to Roman's car, he sighed and looked at the sign above the door.

"Dog's Landing" was etched in thick wood and painted a bright teal. The shop looked like a free-for-all type of store, not unlike many he'd seen in his life.

When he walked in, he realized it wasn't actually like any he'd seen before. While most shops like this were cluttered and unorganized, this one was spotless. Its narrow aisles were neatly filled with groceries, gifts, and everything one would need on a vacation stay in the area, including bait and fishing tackle.

Walking up to the counter, he smiled at the pretty brunette behind the counter.

"Can I help you?"

"I hope so." He glanced at her name tag. "Jenny. I'm looking for my brother, Roman."

She smiled and nodded. "He's helping Missy out on the boats today." Cole felt his fingers start to tingle.

"Missy? Marissa?" His voice sounded hollow.

When Jenny nodded, he felt a wave of relief rush through him, followed quickly by anger. "Where can I find him?" he asked between clenched teeth.

Jenny blinked and looked around. "Um, the boat should be coming back"—she looked down at her watch—"in about ten minutes."

He nodded and left the store without another word. He stepped out on the large deck of the pier, reached in his pocket for his phone, and dialed Marcus.

"Hey." Hearing his brother's voice helped calm him a little.

"You'll never believe where I am."

"Aren't you back from Hawaii yet?"

"Yes, I'm in Carrabelle, chasing down our crazy brother, who appears to have found Marissa."

"What?" Cole could hear he had his brother's full attention. "Have you seen her?"

"No, not yet." The phone was silent for a while.

"Maybe you should come back."

"What?" Cole blinked a few times.

"Listen, if Roman hasn't called to tell us that he's found Marissa, maybe he has a good reason."

Cole shook his head, not sure if he was hearing Marcus right. "Are you nuts?"

"Maybe he's trying to convince her not to get spooked away again."

He thought about it and felt his heart skip. Damn, why

hadn't he thought of it? Marissa might still be running from whatever had caused her to leave all those years ago, and if anyone could convince her to come back, it was Roman.

He turned his head when he heard a boat engine. He watched as a ferry made its way slowly towards the dock. Quickly making up his mind, he rushed from the dock and jumped in the car.

"You still there?" he heard Marcus say.

"No, I'm going."

"Good. Give Roman a little more time. At least we know they're both alive and well."

"I think she has a kid," he blurted out.

"What?"

"Marissa. The kid looked just like her." He remembered that expression on the boy's face and knew that's where he'd seen it before. On Marissa's face, years ago, when she'd first come to the Grayton's.

"Well, dang. We were hoping we'd be the first ones."

"First ones what?" he asked as he drove by the little house again.

"To have a kid in the family."

"You're doing what now?" He blinked and stopped at a stop sign.

"We're having a kid." Marcus laughed. "Just found out yesterday."

"Well damn!" He laughed. "Congratulations. I'll be home in a few hours and we'll go out to celebrate."

"Sounds good." He heard Marcus sigh. "I was just hoping we'd wait until after the house was done."

"Not to mention the wedding." Cole chuckled.

"That doesn't matter much." Marcus laughed. "At least to me." Cole laughed.

Four hours into her shift, Wendy watched Cole and Marcus walk into the bar with their arms slung over each other's shoulders. They looked great together. Happy.

"Well, well, well." She smiled at the pair. "Look what the cat dragged in." She leaned across the bar and took the kiss that Cole gave her, then was shocked when Marcus leaned over and planted one on her lips as well.

"We're having a kid." He smiled at her. She felt her heart skip and then she was being hugged from across the bar.

"Does Shelly know I'm having your baby?" she joked as he pulled away, only to have him laugh. "Congratulations." She hugged him back. "This calls for a drink." She walked over and started pouring their favorite drinks.

"Damn straight it does." Cole smiled at her. "Plus, I found Roman, who apparently has really found Marissa this time."

"What?" They all jumped when Cassey screamed it from the other side of the almost empty room. "Just when in the hell were you going to tell me?" She marched across the room, her hands on her hips.

Cole recoiled and then hid behind Marcus.

"Cole Stephan Grayton." Cassey stopped right in front of him. "Where are they?"

Cole's eyes went to Marcus for help. Marcus stepped in front of his sister and took her shoulders in his hands.

"Cass give Roman time to convince Marissa to come

home."

"I will not!" She tried to push his arms away, so she could wipe away the tears that were streaming down her face.

"Honey, he hasn't actually told us," Cole started to say, but when his sister glared at him, he stopped talking and reached for his drink instead.

"Where are they?" she asked Marcus.

"Just down the coast a way. Promise me you won't tell Julie or dad just yet."

"Where?" she asked again, crossing her arms over her chest.

Marcus just shook his head and then smiled. "We're having a baby."

Wendy watched Cassey's eyes go from mad to happy quickly. "You..." She blinked and swallowed. "Shelly's..."

He nodded, then hugged her tightly and winked at Wendy who just laughed.

For the rest of the evening, the three of them sat at the bar instead of the back booth. At eight, Shelly walked in, looking a little tired. Marcus rushed over and hugged her, spinning her around in circles.

He almost carried her over to the bar stool, where he ordered her dinner and they sat and ate together. Cole shared some fish tacos with her while they watched the news on the upcoming hurricane.

Hurricane Donna was due to arrive on Thursday. So far, it was set to be a category two, which meant that most everyone who lived there year-round would be sticking it out. Some people evacuated for every small storm, but not her.

"So, we'll just have a party then?" Shelly asked, sounding a little concerned.

"Don't worry, honey. There's no real danger if we're someplace safe." Marcus hugged her. "It's her first hurricane," he said to the group who smiled.

"This will be my tenth," Wendy said, laughing.

"Ten?" Cole glanced at her and thought. "I guess that's about right."

She shook her head. "I'm sure you lose track of all the times you've hit the water in a big storm."

He smiled. "Which reminds me…" He held up his finger and took out his phone to make a call.

She leaned on the counter and watched him persuade someone to come visit during the storm.

"Who was that?" she asked when he walked back over to the bar.

"Deyon."

Her eyebrows shot up in question. "*Deyon*?"

He smiled and nodded. "He's been hounding me for a rematch since he was sure someone grabbed his board in the surf, so I told him about the storm and he's coming down." He smiled.

"You are not going to be out in the water when it hits, are you?" Shelly asked, her eyes going big.

He shrugged his shoulders. "It's what I do." He smiled at Shelly.

Wendy turned around and tried to keep busy so she could keep her mind off of what she wanted to say to him. She thought about duct tape, rope, even getting some handcuffs, but knew better since he'd just talk his way out of it. There was nothing she could do to stop him from hitting the water the second the waves started getting big.

CHAPTER 18

Cole watched the waves from the boardwalk and itched to grab his board. Deyon had texted him that he was half an hour away, so he was waiting to hit the water with him. In waves like this, you always took someone along, even if it wasn't someone you liked. Trust was the key factor here and Cole trusted that if anything went wrong, Deyon could be professional about it.

He heard the loud music from the bar behind him, and when he stepped in, he glanced over and saw Willow, Wendy's sister, sitting at the bar, laughing at something her sister had said.

Wendy had filled him in on their conversation and how she felt like everything was mended between them. He sighed and wished that Roman had returned his calls instead of texting the vague message.

-Heard you stopped by. Thanks for not sticking around. Give her some time. She's warming up to the idea of coming home soon. R

"How's it looking out there?" Carl asked, slapping him on his back. His photographer was all dressed up in his diving suit, just like Cole was.

Carl was one of the best storm photographers around, and he'd been lucky enough to catch him before he'd booked a flight to South Africa.

"It's warming up nicely." He rubbed his hands together and smiled. "Just waiting on Deyon."

Carl nodded and then walked over to sit down in a booth to talk to a few other storm surfers, who'd arrived earlier that day. Everyone would head out as a team and keep their eyes on one another.

He walked over to the bar and smiled at Wendy, who was biting her bottom lip and looking very worried.

He tried not to chuckle. He'd spent the last two days trying to convince her that this was nothing big. After all, he was in his own backyard, doing something he loved. Besides, it was only a category two. The waves wouldn't be as big as the ones he'd surfed in Hawaii two years ago during the tropical storm.

That little bit of information didn't help soothe her, nor had the fact that Deyon would be his wingman.

"I don't like that man. Maka told me what he did to you." She'd crossed her arms and glared at him, only to have him laugh.

"Yeah, but that was years ago. I've gotten him back for it. He's still an ass to my face, but he doesn't pull stunts like that."

She'd just glared at him until he'd kissed her senseless and changed the subject.

Just then the front doors opened and Deyon walked in.

All the other surfers jumped up from the booth and cheered, and then they quickly gathered their gear and started towards the door.

Deyon walked towards the bar, smiling.

"The damn taxi didn't want to bring me all the way here." He laughed. "Told me there was a hurricane coming."

Cole chuckled and held out his hand. This time, Deyon took it warmly in his. Competitions were different. Riding a storm was for fun and all egos were put aside.

"Glad you could make it." Cole smiled.

"Had to. Can't let you show me up outside of competitions, too." He chuckled. "Of course, that wouldn't have happened…" Deyon started his spiel about his board being grabbed as they started to head out.

"Hang on a sec," Cole said and everyone groaned. "Just a sec," he yelled as he rushed back behind the bar and kissed Wendy until he felt all of his nerves rush out of his body. "I'll be right back." He smiled and ran to catch up to the rest of the group.

"I can't believe they're going out in that," Willow said as she sighed, watching the surfers head out in the rain.

"It's what they do," Wendy said, not completely feeling convinced herself. She wanted more than anything to argue about it, but so far, Cole had sidestepped the conversations or had tried to convince her that he'd be completely safe.

So she just stayed busy during the party in order to

keep her mind off of the million and one dangers he and his buddies could be facing. There was actually a good crowd growing inside, which kept her busy enough. Especially since she was the only bartender there. Alan had driven down to stay with a friend during the storm, and the rest of the crew had bailed out of state to wait it out in safety. Willow had shown up just after it started raining outside, which had been a big relief.

Cassey and Luke were upstairs in her office, while Marcus and Shelly had decided to wait for the storm out at the Grayton's across the bay. Cole and Cassey had both been relieved that their brother would be there to watch out for their dad and Julie.

The music had been cranked up to drown out the sound of the rain and wind. Wendy watched as Cassey and Luke walked down the stairs a few minutes after Cole and his friends had left. Cassey walked over to the bar, frowning.

"When did they leave?" she nodded to the empty booth.

"About ten minutes ago. Why?"

She shrugged her shoulders. "Just wanted to say…" She shook her head. "Tell him good luck."

Wendy smiled and took her friend's hand. "I know." She shook her head. "If this storm doesn't knock some sense into him, I will." She chuckled and felt her hands shake in Cassey's, who squeezed them.

"He's a pro at this." She chuckled. "Rode out his first storm when he was only seventeen." She sighed. "Of course, Mom was alive, and she swore she'd kill him if he ever did anything like that again." She smiled.

"I thought I could change him." She shook her head.

Cassey laughed. "Sorry, honey, Cole isn't going to change unless Cole decides he needs to change."

Maka's words flashed into Wendy's mind.

"One day, he will ride a wave and decide that it's not enough. That he's still missing something."

She'd hoped that she was what he'd been missing, but since they were in a relationship and he hadn't even slowed down, she doubted he would anytime soon. It made her sad to think about it. She hadn't asked for a commitment from him, but she had hoped for one.

Less than an hour later, the news station updated the storm to a category three, which meant the winds were stronger than they had first thought.

They could hear the howling and the patter of the rain hitting the outside. Since they weren't in the direct path of the storm, it sounded like a normal storm to everyone inside the building. Luke and Marcus had secured the storm shutters the day before, so it was a lot darker inside than normal at this time of day.

Right after they had gotten the update on the news, the front doors opened, and a bunch of surfers rushed in.

"It's too crazy out there," one of them complained. "You'd have to be nuts to stay out there."

Wendy instantly knew that Cole wouldn't be with the group and her heart sank a little. She glanced around and noticed that Deyon and Carl were the only three still out there.

She stayed busy with the storm surfers who had decided it was more fun to get loaded and play pool than try and kill themselves in the storm. With the wind howling outside, she kept her mind occupied by talking to her sister or serving up drinks. She'd even had a beer herself when Cassey had demanded she relax a little.

When the doors opened again, almost an hour later, she felt her heart skip. Then it stopped completely when she noticed that only two people walked through the doors.

"Where's Cole?" Cassey rushed to the door.

Carl wiped the water from his face and frowned. "We got separated. That's why we're back here." He frowned and looked around. "We thought he'd be back by now. The current dragged us a mile up the coast."

Cassey glanced back at her and Wendy held onto the countertop, which was holding her up at this point.

"We'll go back out and see if we can find him," Deyon said, setting his surfboard along the wall with the rest of them.

"I'll go with you." Carl and two others stood up.

"No, not you." Cassey pointed to one man. "You've had a few too many beers. We don't need someone else wandering off."

"I'll go." Another man stood up and Cassey glanced at Wendy, who nodded when she remembered the kid had only been drinking soda.

"Okay." She nodded.

"Let's meet back here in ten minutes," Carl said, glancing at his watch.

As they left, Cassey made her way back towards the bar.

"I'm sure he's on his way back here. Like they said, the current dragged them a mile down the shore."

She nodded and then glanced down, trying to hide her tears of fear. "I'll…" She looked around and noticed that they were low on limes. "I'll just run to the back and cut some more limes." She grabbed the container and rushed from the room blindly.

When she made it to the back fridge, she leaned against the cool door and took a couple deep breaths. What had she gotten herself into? She'd known going into the relationship that it would end like this.

Even if Cole walked through those doors right now, she had to admit to herself that she couldn't handle being with someone like him. Not after growing up with her father. She wouldn't—no, couldn't—put herself through that again.

When she felt the tears streak down her face, she cursed herself for exposing her heart so easily. This is why she had avoided him for years. She'd known he was trouble.

Using her sleeve to clean her face, she closed her eyes and desperately wished for some fresh air. Setting the container of limes down, she opened the cooler and stepped out. Still hearing the wind and rain, she opened the back door and smiled when she noticed she could just stand under the overhang to the side and not get wet. When the door shut behind her, she sighed and felt herself steady a little more.

The back parking lot was almost flooded. Her Jeep sat in its spot with the hardcover protecting the inside from the water. Her mind flashed back to Cole driving Maka's Jeep up the bumpy trail in Hawaii.

Closing her eyes, she leaned against the brick building and wished more than anything that they could go back to the way they were on that trip.

When she heard something crack, she looked around and noticed that the thick wood board that was holding the huge back awning up had cracked. Since the wind was whipping the material around pretty rough, she took a few steps back.

She was about to head back inside when the board came crashing down towards her. She didn't even have time to scream.

CHAPTER 19

Cole coughed up water and cursed himself for not paying attention to the shoreline. This was his backyard, and he knew by just looking at the beach that he was a good four miles down shore.

When he finally escaped the rip current and made his way back to shore, he was another half a mile down. The waves were a lot bigger now and he was still itching to ride, but when he noticed that Carl and Deyon were nowhere to be seen, he knew he had to head back to Cassey's.

After half an hour of walking in the wind and rain, he was really cursing himself. The storm had obviously grown and even with his wetsuit on, he felt a shiver run up his bones.

He carried his board over his head for a while, hoping that would stop some of the water from falling in his face. Instead, it just made his arms ache and his back hurt by the time he made it to the edge of town.

When he finally made it back to the boardwalk, he was

relieved to see Carl standing out front, glancing down the boardwalk.

"Hey," he called out and jogged over to his friend. "Glad you made it back."

Carl spun around and looked a little relieved. "Yeah, you too." He shook his hand.

"Come on, let get inside." He started to walk in.

"You go. I've got to wait for the ambulance."

"Ambulance? For whom?"

"Some girl stepped outside and got cold conked by flying debris."

"Who?" Cole's heart skipped a beat.

Carl shrugged his shoulders and glanced back down the boardwalk. "I don't know. We were out looking for you, and then I was told to wait out here to help the guys find the place."

Cole rushed inside and saw a group of people gathered around one of the tables. Cassey was leaning over someone and when he rushed over, he saw Wendy lying there, unconscious, as Luke held a bloody towel on her forehead.

He must have screamed because everyone looked up at him quickly and moved aside. When he took her hand in his, he noticed how cold she was.

"Blankets," he yelled to his sister. "She's frozen."

Cassey nodded and rushed up the stairs.

"I just found her," Willow cried. "She'd walked off after she heard you had disappeared, and she hadn't come back." Willow wiped the tears from her eyes. "She was crying and I went to check on her, but she wasn't in the cooler."

He was rubbing Wendy's bare arms as Willow talked.

When he looked up, he noticed that Wendy's sister was soaking wet and shivering.

"Where was she?" he asked, gently pushing some of her hair away from the wound as Luke held a towel over her forehead to stop the bleeding.

When Luke replaced the towel with a clean one, he noticed a large gash across her forehead. The sight of it made his knees go weak.

"How long ago did you call the ambulance?"

Luke glanced at his watch. "About fifteen minutes ago."

"She's been out that long?"

"Longer," Willow said. "She'd been missing for about twenty minutes before I went to look for her."

He cursed and closed his eyes and leaned down closer to her. With his lips right next to her ear, he whispered, "If you wake up from this, I promise never to leave your side again." He placed a kiss on her cheek and watched as his tears spilled down onto her skin.

"Here." Cassey rushed back over with a large purple blanket. He quickly pulled her wet shirt up and then ripped it right down the front, leaving her in only her bra. Then he used another towel to dry her wet skin and covered her with the thick blanket. His hands worked over her pale skin, which had turned a light shade of blue from the cold.

"Get her shoes off," he barked, not even looking down at her feet. He knew someone would work on them and cover her completely with the blanket.

By the time the ambulance workers walked in the door, soaking wet, they had warmed her up enough that he felt she no longer had hypothermia.

Then they covered her with waterproof blankets and carted her out, with him on their heels.

"I'll keep you posted," he called back to his sister, who only nodded as she cried into her husband's chest.

The ride to the hospital seemed to take forever. They had to sidestep a few downed power lines, which had eaten up almost fifteen minutes. When they pulled into the hospital, Wendy had still not regained consciousness.

Cole had sat beside her, talking to her in a calm tone, promising her everything he could think of if she would just open her eyes.

Wendy felt like she was floating towards a bright, warm light. She felt her entire body relax into the wave that carried her out to the abyss. At first, there had been nothing but cold and darkness, then the calm had come, and she'd relished the peacefulness. She'd actually actively sought it out by looking towards the light and trying to float closer.

Warm hands rushed over her, a soothing voice called out to her, and she moved closer to the peace. There was nothing on her mind other than obtaining enlightenment.

Then she was spinning in a storm, being pulled down in a whirlwind and sucked under. She found it hard to breathe and cried out as a million needles picked at her skin, ripping it from her bones. Dizziness overtook her and she felt her head spinning faster than she could maintain.

Feeling her stomach revolt, she sat straight up and released her stomach. Warm hands reached out and pushed her back down as soothing hands brushed over her face and eyes.

When she tried to open her eyes, there was only darkness. Crying out, she only calmed down when a voice spoke right next to her ear.

"I'm here. Hold still baby. Everything is going to be okay. Don't fight it. Relax."

She let her body relax completely, and her mind sank back into the darkness until Cole's voice woke her once more.

"Come on, Wendy, open those eyes," he cried next to her ear.

When she did, it was still dark, and she reached out for him.

"Cole?" Her voice sounded so far away.

"I'm here baby. Hold on to me. No—" His hands covered her arms. "Stay still. You're okay. We're at the hospital now." He held her still. "They're moving you to a private room."

"Cole," she cried out again, blinking frantically. "I can't see."

It was silent, and she heard someone speaking quietly to him. "It's okay, it's probably just temporary. They say the hit to your head has caused a lot of swelling." His voice sounded strained. Then she heard his soft cries and reached out for him.

She felt herself being wheeled into another room and shivered when the cool air hit her.

"Can she have another blanket?" Cole asked quickly.

A few minutes later, a blanket was being put on her.

"Willow is here," Cole said next to her. "She wanted to wait since they'll only let one of us back here at a time."

She tried to nod her head, only to realize that she'd been strapped down to a board.

"Okay," she said. "Tell her I'm okay. I… I don't want to see her until… Don't tell her…"

She felt him take her hand and squeeze it. "I'll go tell her that you're awake and will talk to her in a while."

She closed her eyes and sighed. She heard him leave the room and when the door opened again, she heard someone move around the room.

"Hello, Miss Grant. I'm Dr. Zayas. I heard you had a nasty bump." She heard him walk towards her and for the first time in her life, she didn't know what her future would hold.

Cole stepped out into the waiting room and walked slowly towards Willow, who glanced up at him with worried eyes that matched Wendy's perfectly.

He sat next to her. "She's awake." He watched Willow take a deep breath.

"And?" she asked, wiping a tear from her face.

"The doctor will be in to see her soon."

Willow nodded. "Can I see her?"

He shook his head. "Better wait. She wants to see you after they've cleaned her up."

Willow sighed. "I don't know why she keeps babying me." She crossed her arms over her chest and frowned at him. "I'm not a baby. For god's sake, I'm the one that found her."

He sighed and battled with himself about going against Wendy's wishes and telling Willow that Wendy may never see again. God, just the thought of that tore him apart. Especially since he started thinking that if he hadn't gone storm surfing, none of this would have happened.

She had probably gone outside because she'd been upset that he hadn't returned. He groaned and leaned his head back, closing his eyes to the pain.

"Hey." Willow rested her hand on his arm. "Is everything okay?"

He blinked and looked at her, then started to nod his head, but shook it instead. "Willow, Wendy didn't want me to tell you this, but…" He took a deep breath. "When she woke up, she couldn't see."

Willow's hands went to cover her mouth as her eyes got huge. "What does that mean? Is it permanent?"

He shook his head. "I don't know."

She glanced around the room and then stood up. "Well, go find out. I'll wait here. Go talk to the doctor. Don't leave her in there all by herself." She pushed his shoulders until he started walking back towards the doors.

When he walked back into the room, he was surprised to see a doctor shining a flashlight into her eyes.

"Hey." He rushed over to the older man.

"Hi." He smiled up at him. "Dr. Zayas." He held out a hand and Cole shook it. "I'm a big fan of yours."

Cole nodded. "Is she going to be okay?"

The doctor looked down at her and patted her shoulder. "Just a nasty concussion. We're going to give her a few stitches after we x-ray that head of hers." He smiled. "But I think the blindness is only temporary. We'll give it a few days, let the swelling go down, and wait it out." He patted her again on the shoulder. "Now, if you'll excuse me, I'll go get everything set up for her x-ray."

Cole followed the doctor out and stopped him. "Doctor?"

The man turned around and smiled. "Like I said, we won't know anything until the swelling goes down. I'll be around if you have any other questions."

Cole nodded and followed a nurse back into Wendy's room.

"Well?" Wendy asked.

Cole shrugged his shoulders and walked over to her. "He just told me the same thing."

She sighed. "Okay, so we wait."

CHAPTER 20

*L*ate that night, after the worst of the storm was over, Marcus and Shelly arrived along with Cassey and Luke. Wendy could tell everyone had been prepped on her condition since everyone was very quiet when they came in.

She could smell the flowers before someone finally mentioned that they had brought them.

"They smell wonderful," she said, holding out her hands until finally a vase was put in her hands. She buried her face in them and took a deep breath.

When it hit her that she may never see the beauty of a flower again, she started crying and the room grew even quieter.

"They've all stepped outside," Cole said, pulling her close to his side.

"I'm sorry." She sighed next to him. "It's just…"

"I know—" he interrupted. "It's okay."

She sighed again and listened to the steady beat of his heart. "I'm scared."

She felt him nod his head. "Me too."

The door to her room opened again, and she heard Marcus cough.

"Sorry, Cole, I need to borrow you for a moment." His voice sounded strained.

Cole stood up. "I'll be right back." He leaned down, and she felt a kiss on her cheek.

A few minutes later when Cole came back in, he was quiet for a while.

"Is everything okay?" she asked, holding out her hand for him. He walked across the floor and took it and she could feel the tension in his hand.

"It's my brother."

"Roman?"

"Yes."

"What about him?"

"He's missing."

"What?" She sat up a little. "How do you know?"

"My sister called Marcus."

"Cassey?" She frowned, not really understanding.

"No." She felt him shaking. "Marissa."

She blinked a few times. "Where?" She knew he would understand her question.

"He went out looking for... Marissa's son."

"What?"

Cole sat next to her in the bed and sighed as he wrapped his arm around her shoulder. "The kid took off, I guess, and Roman went to find him. Marissa doesn't know where they are now. Marcus and Luke are going to help look for them."

She reached for his hand and brought it up to her lips

like he'd often done to her. "Go, go help them. It's your nephew and brother." She smiled. "I'll be fine here."

He hugged her closer. "I love you," he whispered as she felt a tear slide down her cheek. "I shouldn't have gone." He took a deep breath.

"Cole." She reached up and took his face in her hands, wishing more than anything that she could see his silver eyes. "I love you too. Now go. Find your family." She smiled and leaned forward until his lips found hers.

After he'd gone, Willow sat with her and held her hand.

"I'm sorry about everything," her sister said, squeezing her hand.

"Everything?" she joked. "Like… the time you threw my hairbrush into the spaghetti bowl? Or the time you replaced my eyeliner with a permanent marker?"

Willow laughed. "Okay, not everything. You totally deserved those."

"Right." Wendy smiled. "And you deserved it when I picked you up from school wearing a Darth Vader mask and singing 'Turning Japanese' loudly."

Willow laughed even harder. "Okay, I totally deserved that."

She leaned down and hugged her, and Wendy knew that no matter what happened, everything would be all right as long as she had her family.

Cole was wet and tired, not to mention worried beyond anything he'd ever felt. They had searched all night just outside of Carrabelle, which had been hit a lot harder than

Surf Breeze had. The small town he'd driven through was pretty much just a pile of rubble.

He'd cried when he'd seen Marissa, and so had Marcus and Cassey, who had stayed behind with Marissa while Cole went out to help with the search. There were over two dozen people looking for their brother, along with Marissa's seven-year-old son Reagan.

When Cole was too tired to take another step, Marcus had told him to take a break while he kept searching. Cole had gotten a ride back to the hospital in Panama City. When he got to Wendy's room, he found Willow sitting in a chair, leaning to one side with her head falling forward. He helped her move to the empty bed next to the window, so she could get some real rest.

Instead of sitting up in the chair that Willow had just vacated, he walked over and gently moved Wendy's sleeping body over a little, then lay next to her in her bed and quickly fell asleep with her in his arms.

He didn't move until he felt her shift above him. When he opened his eyes, he saw her smiling down at him and he smiled back.

"Hi," he said, closing his eyes and resting his forehead next to hers, pulling her closer.

"Morning." She chuckled.

Then it dawned on him as he remembered the horrors of the day before. His eyes flew open again as he took in her entire face. Her eyes ran over his face and locked in on his eyes.

He saw her smile and nod slowly. "I can see," she said, causing him to kiss her firmly and pull her closer.

"Ouch." She giggled. "Okay, easy on the old noodle

here." Her hand went to her head as he apologized and kissed her more gently.

"Sorry." He chuckled as he watched Willow sit up in the bed next to them.

Wendy followed his gaze and cried as her sister rushed to her and hugged her.

An hour later, after he'd grabbed a quick hospital shower, he was ready to catch a ride back to Carrabelle to join the search party again. He hated leaving Wendy, but she was being released from the hospital later that day. Willow had agreed to drive her home and stay with her until he could return.

"I'll be home when you get done." She kissed him, her hands going into his hair.

"I like the sound of that." He smiled and held onto her.

"What?" She glanced up at him.

"Home." He kissed her again.

"Good, because I don't plan on living in a one-room condo for long." She sighed.

He sighed right after her. "Maybe we should have that talk." He frowned down at her, his eyes going narrow.

"What talk?" She frowned, matching his mood.

"The 'how many kids do you want' talk." He smiled, loving the sound of her chuckle.

She smiled. "How about the 'I'm finished risking my life' talk?"

He nodded, and his smile fell away. "There is no need to talk about it."

Her heart spiraled down to her stomach. Then he took her hands and pulled her close.

"I'm retiring. I've found my purpose." He kissed her. "It's you."

She felt a tear slide down her cheek. He reached up and wiped it away with his finger.

"Come back soon." She smiled.

He nodded. "I'll be home as quickly as I can." He kissed her again, and she nodded and then let him go.

issy leaned against the counter and swayed her hips to the old tune that was pumping out of the small speakers she'd hung up the week before. The short shorts she was wearing were a little too old and loose, but she didn't care, not when the music was taking her back to the good ol' days.

Images flashed in her mind as she punched the keys to the old ten-key calculator. She smiled when she saw that she was under budget again this month, but she would work the numbers once more just to make sure.

It still got her deep in her chest when she saw the extra money sitting in her bank account after everything was paid at the end of the month. Smiling, she looked up as one of her employees, Jenny, walked in.

The girl was young and pretty enough to keep customers happy, even when they found out they would have to pay a little more than at some of the other places along the Gulf shore.

White-sugar-sand beaches sat right outside of Dog's

Landing's front door, along with the long dock that housed three of her best moneymakers. One boat was a ferry, which could carry five full-size cars to Dog Island, along with over a dozen passengers. One of the other boats was smaller but made just about as much money as the ferry did carrying parasailers across the crystal-clear waters of the Gulf. Her last boat was bigger and made the most money by taking a group of eight out into the deeper waters on fishing charters.

Buying the two other boats had been one of the first changes she'd made when she'd inherited the small convenience store, along with the dock and the old ferryboat.

It had been a shock at first, running her own business, but she'd adjusted like she always had in life.

Sighing, she stood up and watched Jenny straighten a few cans of food and boxes of cereal as she made her way towards the back of the store. Her long blonde hair swayed with each step she took. Her standard uniform of shorts and a button-up blouse made Missy remember she had wanted to go clothes shopping for a few new items.

"Sorry, I'm late." Jenny smiled as she walked around the counter.

Missy laughed. "Jenny, you're never late." She glanced at the clock and smiled. "Actually, you're five minutes early."

Jenny sighed. "I'm late if I'm not ten minutes early."

Missy shook her head at her. "I just can't understand it."

Jenny leaned against the counter and giggled. "My granny taught me well."

"Wish I could say the same about all my other employees." She frowned when she noticed that the smallest of her boats were still docked outside. There were customers waiting out on the docks for their turn to enjoy flying over the water. "Where are Tom and Roger?" She sighed and knew it was past time to get more reliable employees to run the parasailing tours.

"Where do you think?" Jenny picked up the shop phone and dialed. "Hey, yeah, again." She rolled her eyes. "Okay. Thanks."

Missy crossed her arms over her chest and watched Jenny hang up the phone. "You can't keep asking them to do this."

Jenny smiled. "I know, but they like it."

"He's old. They're too old."

Jenny laughed. "Not as old as you think."

"I don't know how those two can keep up with people half their age."

Jenny smiled and shrugged her shoulders. "They tell me working here keeps them young."

Missy laughed. "Right." Just then they both turned to see Jenny's grandfather, John, and his best friend, Bob, walk in. Both men were in shorts and smiling from ear to ear.

The men lived less than a block from the store and had been a staple in both Carrabelle, Florida, and to Dog's Landing since before she'd been born.

"Good thing you called. We were driving the wives stir-crazy." Bob chuckled as he walked over and grabbed the boat keys from behind the countertop.

"Full day?" John asked.

She nodded. "You're booked solid. Unless Tom and Roger show up, it's all yours for the day."

As the men glanced at each other then walked out

chuckling, Jenny leaned closer. "You know they make more in tips than Tom and Roger."

She sighed and nodded. "Yeah, it's funny when two old men can out-earn two young hunks."

Jenny laughed. "Tom and Roger are not hunks. They're dorks."

Missy frowned and tilted her head. "I wish you would have told me that when I hired them."

"I did." She laughed. "Trust me, next time, let me do the hiring."

She nodded. "Okay, it's all yours." There were still things she was learning about the business, even after five years of running it.

"I'm going to head out on the next ferry ride. I've got a few deliveries." She nodded to the cart full of boxes, which were stuffed with orders.

The store had many customers who lived on Dog Island in St. George Sound, one of Florida's only totally secluded islands. There was a small airstrip on the island, but most of the locals used her ferry service to move between the island and the mainland. Many of the people who lived on the island were pretty self-reliant. There were fewer than three dozen homes on the semi-private island and she had almost a dozen loyal customers who helped keep her doors open and her shelves stocked with groceries.

Dog's Landing had been delivering groceries to the Islanders since she'd taken over the store. The customers loved that their food was delivered fresh daily and she loved the work.

"Enjoy it. I hear we're supposed to have some bad weather later this week." Jenny leaned down and pulled out a fresh bottle of water from the stocked fridge behind the counter.

"Yeah." She frowned. "Already I've had a few cancellations for fishing trips."

Jenny shrugged her shoulders. "I'll bet it will pass quickly. It always does this time of year. Then, you watch. We'll be booked solid for the Fourth of July."

Missy smiled as she loaded the small handcart full of the deliveries. "Yeah, remember last year?" She laughed. "The two groups that fought over the charter boat." She laughed, remembering how the two groups had tried to outbid one another for the day use of her boat.

"We could hire another boat this year," Jenny said, looking over the schedule book. "We're already booked, but I bet we could easily book another boat solid for that weekend."

She tilted her head. "Do you know someone?"

Jenny smiled. "I don't, but I bet my grandfather would. I can ask him when he comes in for lunch."

Missy thought about it and nodded. "While you're at it if he knows anyone else to hire…"

Jenny laughed. "I'll ask. If Tom and Roger show up?"

She sighed and closed her eyes. "I guess I need to go ahead and rip that Band-Aid off as well."

Jenny smiled. "I'll do it. Don't worry. I already have one person in mind for replacing them. I'll have to look around for another." She frowned.

"You are too good to me." Missy smiled. "I don't know what I would do without you."

"Good thing you pay me well." She smiled at their private joke. "Now, you'd better get going. The ferry is coming in." She nodded towards the front windows. Sure enough, the big boat was making its way towards the dock.

By the time Missy had carted out the two loads of boxes and the large cooler for her deliveries, the ferry was already filled up with new passengers and cars.

She waved up to Clay, one of the ferry captains. Clay and Marv, two men who had worked as ferry master for the past eight years, usually alternated workdays. She allowed them to make their own schedules since it tended to work best when they communicated with one another directly. She didn't mind, so long as there was someone manning the ferry seven days a week.

She stored the supplies and locked them down for the half-hour journey to the island, and then she made her way up to sit next to Clay.

"Hey," she sighed as he started pulling the ferry away from the dock.

"Hey." He smiled over at her. Clay was easily one of the sexiest men she knew. But all the women around knew that Clay's wife of almost ten years, and his high school sweetheart, was eight and a half months pregnant. "Do you have a lot of deliveries today?" He glanced over at her quickly and she wished more than anything that she could find someone that would cause her heart to skip who didn't have a gold band around his finger.

She shrugged her shoulders. "It might take me a while." She rolled her eyes. "Mrs. Mette has two boxes today."

He chuckled, and she felt her insides kick at the rich sound. She could only ever remember one other person who'd caused her body to respond that way. Sighing, she forced her mind to focus as she glanced below deck at the passengers enjoying the slow ride.

"I don't know why you let that woman push you around like she does."

She smiled. "Well, it helps that she's one of our best customers."

Clay glanced at her again. "And one of the craziest people on Dog Island."

She chuckled. "Yeah, but you have to admit, she gives us something to talk about."

He laughed and nodded and then focused on maneuvering the ferry out of the small port and into the deeper waters of Saint George Sound.

Missy loved the peaceful ride out to the island and back. She even enjoyed riding the small electric cart on the island to deliver the groceries. She really did enjoy everyone on the island, even Mrs. Mette, although it was quite a pain when she happened to be in one of her moods.

Missy shivered at the thought of having to run back to the mainland to replace an item she wasn't satisfied with. One time, it had taken her a full day of running back and forth before Mrs. Mette was satisfied that she had the freshest eggs possible.

By the time she had everything unloaded from the ferry, with the help of Clay, there was a small trail of sweat rolling down her back. She loved living along the Gulf Coast, especially during the summer months.

As she pulled her small electrical cart out of the parking area, she waved at a few locals and hit the small road towards her first delivery. Dog Island was a small community she loved being part of, even though she didn't live on the island herself. She smiled as she pulled up to her first stop and thought of her small cottage a few blocks from the store. She'd been shocked when she'd found it up for sale and had been even more in shock when she'd been approved for the loan. She could remember the countless hours she'd spent as a child dreaming about her future home. This one hadn't disappointed her childhood dreams.

The first few deliveries went quickly and by the time the cart was almost empty, she had to pull over so she could eat the small sandwich and soda she'd packed in the cooler for her lunch. As she sat on the side of the road, people stopped and talked to her as they made their way around the island. There were no posted speed limits, and everyone knew everyone else, which made it easier for her to make her deliveries since people tended to leave their homes unlocked.

Half of her clients left instructions for her to deliver and put away their groceries, which she did without a qualm. But Mrs. Mette was a whole other breed. Even though she should have been her next stop, Missy waited until after she'd delivered the other two deliveries before heading back towards the older woman's house.

Here, on the farthest and most secluded tip of the island, there wasn't a paved road; instead, the sand had been cleared for carts and cars to get through. Most of the homes along this part of the path were accessible by water only. Yet her cart easily made the trek since she'd replaced the smaller tires just last year with larger ones that had high-traction treads. It was a bumpy ride that she couldn't make in bad weather, but she enjoyed it. It was like going four-wheeling or riding in a sand buggy. She loved seeing the white sand kick up behind her as she flew towards the largest house on the island.

Mrs. Mette was in her late sixties and looked like she was at least twenty years older, probably due to the amount of time the woman spent in a bathing suit sitting out by the huge swimming pool in the back of her house.

Her home was far away from anyone else and Missy had it on good authority that Mrs. Mette didn't always bathe with a suit on. She cringed at the thought and took a deep breath, silently praying that today would be one of the woman's saner days.

She pulled the handcart off the back and piled on the two large boxes of Mrs. Mette's items. When she finally made it through the sand to the small boardwalk and up the stairs, Mrs. Mette was already holding the door open for her.

"I was beginning to wonder if you'd forgotten about me." The older woman smiled at her. Missy noted that she was wearing a long silk cover over her suit today. She was thankful that it appeared to be one of her better days.

"No, just a very busy delivery day." She smiled and stopped the cart in front of the door.

"Oh, good. Well, come on in." She held the door open.

It still got to Missy, seeing the amount of wealth this lone woman had. Even though she'd chosen to seclude herself on an island in the Gulf of Mexico and had no car or other means of transportation that Missy knew of, the woman was wealthy beyond belief.

The furniture alone must have cost more than Missy's little cottage home, which she was so very proud of. Italian tile, marble, stone, and some of the richest, warmest woods she'd ever seen filled the more than six-thousand-square-foot place that was this woman's entire world.

The outside of the home looked nothing like the inside.

Outside, the place was plain, boring. It was a fairly square home with a large deck and pool off the back. The metal roof was a bright gold, matching the yellowish tint of the walls. There were lots of windows, and each one had storm shutters in case of high winds.

But inside, the house could have come straight off the pages of *Better Homes and Gardens, Millionaire Edition.* Large stone columns separated the two largest rooms, and high ceilings made the rooms look even bigger. The front room was decorated in all white. Large white sofas with pale blue fluffed pillows sat facing one another on the marble floors. Thick accent rugs cushioned their footsteps as they walked past the perfect room towards the kitchen area.

There was a large marble dining table, which could easily seat six people, immediately in front of a large island. To say that Mrs. Mette's kitchen was what dreams were made of would have been an understatement.

The first time Missy had seen it, she'd dreamed about it for the rest of that month.

Large, warm wood planks ran along the high ceiling as soon as you passed through the stone archways into the kitchen area. Two large chandeliers hung high over the dining table. Missy just knew that they each cost more than her car.

The kitchen itself was completely white, like the rest of the downstairs. Its high cabinets and stone counter-tops always gleamed. Actually, Missy had never seen anything out of place in the house. Mrs. Mette seemed to not belong in the gleaming cleanliness.

She stopped her cart in front of the bar area and quickly got to work putting each item in its designated spot, noting when she found the woman was low on other items on the checklist she'd created almost six years ago.

"You're running low on wild rice," she said absent-mindedly as she continued to put the items away.

"Yes, I had a few guests over the other night." The woman sighed and leaned against the counter, watching Missy's every move.

"Oh?" She smiled at the woman and jotted down to deliver two more boxes the next trip.

"Yes, well." The woman shook her head and glanced out the window, something Missy had never seen her do before. Mrs. Mette had always kept a very keen eye on her movements when she was there, almost like she didn't trust her to not steal anything or, worse, drop something and make a mess.

"Is everything all right?" she asked, turning to the older woman when she noticed a sad look cross her eyes.

The woman glanced back at her and then blinked a few times. "Yes, of course, it is." She straightened her shoulders and Missy saw that she was back to her old self. She turned back to the task at hand.

"Are you married?" Mrs. Mette asked out of the blue.

For the six and a half years that Missy had been delivering this woman's groceries, she'd never asked her a personal question. Until now.

"No." She frowned as she put away the last can of tomato soup. Then she turned towards Mrs. Mette.

"Have you ever been?" The older woman had her arms crossed over her chest and was leaning back on the marble counter-tops.

Missy shook her head, unsure of what had brought on the line of questioning. Sure, she was friendly with most of the customers she delivered for. Most of them knew her life story and she knew theirs. It wasn't as if she'd been hiding anything from anyone. A deep feeling in her gut made its way to her heart and she felt it skip a beat. Okay, maybe just a few things.

"Why?" She set the empty box back onto her cart and glanced at the older woman again. The woman sighed and glanced out of the window once more.

"It's hard." Her eyes moved towards Missy's. "Living alone. Being alone all the time." She shook her head and Missy thought she saw a tear pool in the corner of her eye before she turned her head to look back out towards the water. "We're not meant for it."

"Mrs. Met—"

"Ruth." The woman turned towards her. "You've been delivering my groceries for how many years?"

Missy blinked. "A little over six."

"And in all that time, you have never once been unkind to me or shown me anything but respect. You should be able to call me by my first name. Ruth."

Missy nodded and smiled. "Ruth are you sure everything is all right?"

Ruth smiled and nodded. "Your first name is Missy, correct?" Missy nodded. "Missy, do me a favor…"

Missy's heart sank as she thought about making another trip back to the mainland to grab an item Ruth had forgotten.

"Don't let life pass you by without letting someone into your life. Someone who'll love you." She turned her head and looked out the window again. "Someone to be there in the silence of the night and hold you tight."

When Ruth's eyes moved back to hers, Missy nodded.

There was a knot deep in her throat, which she tried to swallow the entire trip back to Dog's Landing.

When she walked through the door of the store almost an hour later, she heard Jenny laughing in the back room. Walking towards the sound, she stopped cold when she saw the back of a man's head, leaning over her employee.

"Oh!" she exclaimed and started to turn away. She'd never seen Jenny involved with anyone before, even though she knew the girl had in the past had a few boyfriends.

"Wait." Jenny rushed after her. "It's not like it looked." She giggled. "Roman was just…"

Nothing else Jenny said could get past the loud ringing she heard in her ears.

Roman.

Roman.

She'd just been thinking about her Roman, thanks to the conversation with Ruth.

She blinked a few times when Jenny's fingers dug into her shoulders. Then her hearing returned.

"Are you okay?" Jenny was frowning at her as they stood in the small hallway just outside of the break room.

The knot that had built in her throat from her talk with Ruth had traveled farther south and now sat directly over her heart. Missy's fingers shook. She felt a slight sheen instantly coat her skin as she moved her eyes slowly towards the man who was standing just inside the doorway.

He'd changed. A lot, she thought, just as everything faded to white.

ISBN: 978-1-942896-04-3

PRINT ISBN: 978-1-514738-65-8

Copyeditor: Erica Ellis – inkdeepediting.com

Missy's Moment

Breaking Travis

Roping Ryan

Wild Bride

Corey's Catch

Tessa's Turn

The Grayton Series

Last Resort

Someday Beach

Rip Current

In Too Deep

Swept Away

High Tide

Lucky Series

Unlucky In Love

Sweet Resolve

Best of Luck

A Little Luck

Silver Cove Series

Silver Lining

French Kiss

Happy Accident

Hidden Charm

A Silver Cove Christmas

Entangled Series – Paranormal Romance

The Awakening

The Beckoning

The Ascension

Haven, Montana Series

Closer to You

Never Let Go

Holding On

Pride Oregon Series

A Dash of Love

My Kind of Love

Season of Love

Tis the Season

Dare to Love

Where I Belong

Wildflowers Series

Summer Nights

Summer Heat

Stand Alone Books

Twisted Rock

For a complete list of books:

http://JillSanders.com

ABOUT THE AUTHOR

Jill Sanders is a New York Times, USA Today, and international bestselling author of Sweet Contemporary Romance, Romantic Suspense, Western Romance, and Paranormal Romance novels. With over 55 books in eleven series, translations into several different languages, and audiobooks there's plenty to choose from. Look for Jill's bestselling stories wherever romance books are sold or visit her at jillsanders.com

Jill comes from a large family with six siblings, including an identical twin. She was raised in the Pacific Northwest and later relocated to Colorado for college and a successful IT career before discovering her talent for writing sweet and sexy page-turners. After Colorado, she decided to move south, living in Texas and now making her home along the Emerald Coast of Florida. You will find that the settings of several of her series are inspired by her time spent living in these areas. She has two sons and off-set the testosterone in her house by adopting three furry little ladies that provide her company while she's locked in her writing cave. She enjoys heading to the beach, hiking, swimming, wine-tasting, and pickleball with her husband, and of course writing. If you have read any of her books, you may also notice that there is a love of food, especially sweets! She has been blamed for a few added pounds by her assistant, editor, and fans… donuts or pie anyone?

facebook.com/JillSandersBooks

twitter.com/JillMSanders

bookbub.com/authors/jill-sanders